WICKEDPEDIA

CHRIS VAN ETTEN

POINT HORROR

To the patient, whip-smart editors everywhere, but one in particular. You know who you are (*psst*, Mallory).

No part of this publication may be reproduced, stored in a retrieval system, or transmitted in any form or by any means, electronic, mechanical, photocopying, recording, or otherwise, without written permission of the publisher. For information regarding permission, write to Scholastic Inc., Attention: Permissions Department, 557 Broadway, New York, NY 10012.

ISBN 978-0-545-41587-3

Library of Congress Cataloging-in-Publication Data Available

Copyright © 2014 by Chris Van Etten
All rights reserved. Published by Point, an imprint of Scholastic Inc. SCHOLASTIC, POINT, and associated logos are trademarks and/or registered trademarks of Scholastic Inc.

12 11 10 9 8 7 6 5 4 3 2 1   14 15 16 17 18 19/0

Printed in the U.S.A.   40

First edition, July 2014
Book design by Natalie C. Sousa

University and College Admissions

From *Wickedpedia*, the feared encyclopedia

University admissions or **college admissions** is the process through which students gain admission to universities and colleges. Requirements vary from country to country.

But one thing is common to the process around the world: Competition among prospective enrollees is fierce. Today, applicants are justified in resorting to unconventional measures to set themselves apart from the rest of the pack.

Even murder.

CHAPTER 1

*T*here are tools among us.

This was clear to Cole Redeker as his bus farted its way through a November slush to the entrance of Springfield High School.

Spotting the new BMW in the student parking lot was what cinched it. The driver and his passenger bounced out in sync, their Axe Dark Temptation body spray unfurling around them like fallout. If Josh Truffle and Scott Dare weren't honing their soccer skills, they were popping their collars or buying braided belts. Cole had frittered away his junior high years on the fringe of this duo of mom-anointed "nice boys," manning the midfield and dabbling in the preppier arts, a fact that his friend and personal provocateur, Gavin, would never let him forget.

Back then Cole's mom had signed him up for the summer league in the dual hope that he'd spend less time in the kitchen experimenting with piecrust recipes and instead expand his social circle beyond Gavin, who, at thirteen, had already begun to exhibit certain qualities guidance counselors deemed indicative of the "slacker." Chief among them: playing bass in a terrible jam band. Nothing raises the hackles of the PTA crowd higher than a Grateful Dead cover.

Gavin was honored by her disapproval, and upped the ante every chance he got, purposely leaving hacky sacks at Cole's house for her to find.

"Thanks, Mrs. R!" he said when she offered one up, asking if it was his. "I was wondering where I'd left that. Can't seem to focus these days. Do I smell brownies?"

The friendship had blossomed and Cole's parents learned to tolerate Gavin, if barely, because even the boy's best efforts at corruption could not corrupt their son. Cole still scored straight As, still headlined the debate team, still sat first-chair sax, still trained seeing-eye dogs, still turned water into wine. . . .

"If preparing to get into college was a profession, you'd be CEO."

"It *is* a profession," was Cole's doleful response. His parents had assembled a war council to shepherd him into an Ivy League institution of their choosing: an SAT tutor, a private admissions counselor, and a doctoral candidate hired to edit his college essays. "By the time I get accepted they won't have any money left to pay tuition." Which had a great deal to do with the reason he rode a bus to school instead of cruising up in his own BMW, or perhaps more realistically, a Kia.

A tasteful, nondescript Kia that would get the job done and never, ever draw attention to his connections and wealth, which wasn't a problem, anyway, because he lacked both.

But not for long, he daydreamed. And with good reason. Cole Redeker did not have his own credit card, but he did have goals to spare and the tools to achieve them: brains and patience. Expertly wielded, they would win him acceptance to a top-tier school and a four-year vacation from his parents while he laid the groundwork for his real post-grad plans: a gourmet empire to dwarf any of those charlatans featured on the so-called Food Network. Forget about a BMW. He'd have a Ferrari, a Lamborghini, and an Alfa Romeo — the more vowels the better. The more vowels, the more attention he might attract from a certain ex-girlfriend ("Correction: *only* ex-girlfriend," he could hear Gavin say). But stepping off the bus that cold Monday morning, forced to take an undignified leap over a puddle of sludge, he was confronted with the BMW — its flawless German engineering, moonroof, and leather interior. Suddenly Cole felt that his strategy of focusing on his future was doing his present a grave injustice.

What kind of parents go out and buy their son a brand-new BMW with winter looming, except maybe to rub it in the faces of people whose parents can't?

Tools, that's who.

Gavin's two favorite phrases:

1. "It'll be fun. I promise!"
2. "Told you so."

Cole was fond of neither. The first was usually what Gavin trotted out to tempt Cole into aiding in some mischievous, vaguely criminal act. The second was how Gavin invariably greeted him the day after Cole declined to take part. Often Gavin displayed proof that the so-called fun was had. Examples included: a neck brace, shaved eyebrows, or the dental impression of an alpaca on his butt. Sometimes, however, Gavin's wordplay surprised Cole. Sometimes he switched it up.

"So Josh turned out to be a total Neanderthal? Told you so."

This was not one of those times.

They were on their way to Mr. Drick's honors history, a rare shared class and Gavin's sole academic interest.

"You should've seen it coming," said Gavin. "Remember how you used to be 'friends'? Look at how that turned out. Look at your miserable excuse for a life now."

"I'm aware, thanks," Cole said sharply. He needed no reminder of the humiliation he suffered at Josh's hands. He wore it like a noose.

"Just making sure," said Gavin. "Sometimes it's hard to tell if you're only moping or if that's the new you."

Cole was too distracted to respond. Ambling down the hall ahead of them was Josh, his arm slung over the shoulders of his girlfriend, Winnie. They lingered outside Mr. Drick's room to punish unwitting bystanders with a drooly kiss. Gavin told him to look away. "Why torture yourself?"

"I'm not tortured," Cole answered stiffly. "It doesn't bother me."

Cole had many talents. Lying was not among them.

"How evolved of you," Gavin drawled. "Because bearing witness to those two excavate their esophagi between classes bothers me into a boil. And I'm not even her ex-boyfriend. Josh didn't steal her from me. He stole her from you."

That day, history class passed in a tide of dates and facts, none of which sank in for Cole. His mind was on his personal history, which happened to be seated two desks up and one row over.

Winnie. Concert-choir soloist, all-county tennis player, animal-shelter volunteer.

Winnie. Whose long auburn hair draped across her back in thick vines and hadn't been cut since last year, when Cole suggested she continue to let it grow. "Think of the points you'll score with admissions officers when you finally donate it to Locks of Love," he'd advised.

Winnie. Known once as Cole's first kiss, now as his chief competition for valedictorian and forevermore as his faithless, backstabbing ex-girlfriend.

Winnie. Or, as Gavin dubbed her in the post-breakup era, Whinny. Cole tried to get across that homonym humor worked only written, not spoken, but it didn't matter to Gavin. "It only needs to be funny to me," he explained.

It wasn't funny to Cole. Nothing about Winnie was funny. Not since the eve of the SATs, when the school's underground newspaper broke the story that she'd dumped him — before she'd actually dumped him. At the time, he'd dismissed it as preposterous and e-mailed the reporter his demand for a retraction. The response he got from the mysterious gossip columnist WaldaWinchell@SHSmuckraker.com read:

> I stand by my story. And I stand by you. You
> deserve better. Chin up, Cole. WW

Cole wrote it off. "Psychological warfare," he told Gavin. "Whoever started this rumor wants to knock me off my game before the SATs. It's a joke." He wasn't laughing when Winnie cut him loose at the exam site, then scurried right over to Josh, who awaited her with open arms and No. 2s.

Winnie. The source of the dark circles under his eyes and the cause of his dangerous flirtation with an A-minus average.

That flirtation had become a full-blown affair. As class drew to a close, Mr. Drick returned their graded essays, along with a helping of dandruff. Cole's essay was branded with a big red *B*. Cole was aghast. To him, *B* stood for "Better up your game or it's Ball State for you, bub."

"You're slipping, bro," Gavin hooted after class. "Keep this up and Whinny will grab the top spot right out from under you."

"I'd like to see her try," Cole snapped, stifling the dread that she was nipping at his heels. "She'd have to tear herself away from Josh long enough to study first."

"You do nothing but study. And cook. How's that working out for you?"

"And how did your essay fare?" Cole said, trying to change the subject. "Did Drick find your musings on Benedict Arnold as penetrating as you do?"

"Dunno," he breezed. "I picked up someone else's essay instead. Guess who got an A-plus?" He spotted Josh exiting the classroom, looking around, and he proceeded to read aloud: "'A comparison between American and international serial killers reveals several notable differences.' I wonder what those are. Do you think he's about to tell us?" Alerted, Josh made a beeline for the twosome. Winnie followed, leashed to her boyfriend. Gavin continued his dramatic reading.

"'Perhaps most striking is that when selecting victims, Americans tend to adhere to far more rigid criteria than their worldwide counterparts. An American serial killer knows his victim; an international serial killer *discovers* his victim.' What kind of messed-up mind writes about serial killers for history? Oh, hi, Josh."

"What are you doing with my essay?" Josh demanded to know.

"Just admiring the prose. Mr. Drick thinks it's top-quality work. Care to let us in on your secret?"

Josh snatched his paper. "Keep your hands off my stuff." He looked at Cole looking at Winnie. "That goes for you, too." Cole watched them go.

"Getting in Josh's face like that is just asking for trouble," said Cole. "I don't know why you bother."

"Because someone needs to, and you lack the cojones for the job. Otherwise, watch his cheating wreck the curve for the rest of us."

Cole looked at Gavin askance. "Cheating?"

"Do you really think that essay sprang from his brain? Josh couldn't string two sentences together with barbed wire."

It was the widely held suspicion among SHS students that the administration instructed Josh's teachers to go easy on him. Without his talented feet, the soccer program would be in tatters. Cole didn't doubt that the faculty goosed the curve in his favor, but they'd never abide out-and-out cheating.

"Winnie probably helped him," Cole offered.

"Maybe," Gavin said, slowing by a water fountain. He lowered his voice as a litter of freshmen passed. Safety in numbers. "Or maybe she's cheating, too."

If Cole had been wearing a glove — and living in Victorian England — he'd have slapped Gavin with it and demanded satisfaction. "Winnie does not cheat!"

"Except on you, you mean?"

Cole felt his ribs constrict. "Since when do you care about the curve, anyway? I thought you didn't even want to go to college. Don't you want to take over your dad's mail route or something?"

Gavin kicked a loose pen down the hall. "Mail is going the way of network television and the polar ice caps. What I want is to see justice done. Josh and Winnie committed a crime against you. They turned you into a joke. All you've done since then is wallow. And your cooking hasn't been the same. Last week's cupcakes were seriously subpar."

"You had three."

"Barely! It was all I could do to lick the crusted frosting off the wrappers."

They turned a corner. Josh and Winnie had stopped at a table where tickets to the winter formal were on sale. Cole stared. He and Winnie had ironed out their plans for the party just days before she'd broken up with him. She told him what color dress she was getting. What color corsage to buy. What kind of tux he should rent. He'd smiled and taken notes, just happy to be there.

Now his plans were Josh's.

"You're doing it right now!" Gavin griped.

"Doing what?"

"Brooding." Cole felt his face flush. "Either get over it and move on or don't get over it and get back at them."

The thought had a certain appeal. But he doubted he had the stomach for revenge. "What would I even do?"

Gavin gleamed. "I'm sure we'll come up with something. And it'll be fun. *I promise*."

CHAPTER 2

Gavin

Black magic curse

Next

Shave his eyebrows while he's sleeping

They'll just grow back.

Plant bedbugs in his mattress

Let me just call my good friend the entomologist

Gavin texted revenge scenarios from physics while Cole was holed up in the library.

Enlist him in the army

Sounds like fraud and/or identity theft

None of them were particularly good.

Put hair dye in his shampoo

That could backfire

And make him more irresistible to Winnie

Afraid he's getting further with her than you ever did?

I'm sure they're totally chaste

Just like you two were

Cole didn't take the bait. Ever since he and Winnie had started dating, Gavin had been grubbing around for details. Cole never breathed a word. He told himself it was because he was so honorable, but it might have had something to do with the fact that they'd only ever kissed, though that was more than what perpetually dateless Gavin ever did.

Not that Cole ever complained about kissing. Cole prided himself on a compliment Winnie had paid him after their first kiss at one of Ben Feldman's pool parties, the kind where no one got their hair wet. Cole and Winnie sat on the edge, their toes wriggling in the water as everyone else paired off to claim their own dark corner. Cole and Winnie were left alone with the fireflies. Winnie lifted her legs out of the water, stretching.

"I've got goose bumps."

Suddenly Cole was acutely aware of the way his leg hair bobbed in the water. *Am I too hairy?* he worried. *Not hairy enough? Should I shave my legs? Is there an ancient remedy for not-hairy-enough legs? Do people get leg-hair transplants? What if she looks at my legs? Has she already?* Desperate to lose these thoughts, he surprised them both with a kiss. More surprising: She kissed him back. Afterward, she smiled. "That was nice. Velvety."

Nice. Velvety. Shakespeare couldn't have said it better.

No way she said stuff like that to Josh.

Right?

Cole
Get back to me when you come up with something useful

Cole shut off his phone and settled back into his study carrel, trying to push aside thoughts of Winnie. He was supposed to be working on his oral report for Drick's class. So far he had "The Algonquin Round Table was."

He was about to put pen to paper when he heard the noise.

Somewhere nearby, someone was crying. Crying or choking on a tongue ring — Cole couldn't be sure which. The only experience he had with body piercings was the time he stepped on a thumbtack. He didn't know how choking on a tongue ring might sound, but he imagined it was something like the snuffles wafting through the library's stacks.

Cole peeked out from behind his carrel, angling for the sound's source.

He padded to a seldom-visited aisle, slipped out a volume of German verse, and pretended to look captivated by the abundance of syllables as he eavesdropped. Through the cracks came the whisper-talk of a familiar voice. Winnie.

Walk away, Cole. He edged closer to the stack, absently turning a page in the book he wasn't looking at. Between the shelf and the top of the books he glimpsed a shifting sliver of Winnie. The swoop of her autumn-colored hair, the bat of an eyelash.

She wasn't the one crying, but there was an uncharacteristic tremor in her voice. Cole had never seen or heard Winnie cry, not even the day she tried to teach him her backhand and he accidentally backhanded her face. First she corrected his grip. Then she plugged the blood spurting from her nose. She did not shed a tear when she dumped him for Josh, either. But there, deep in the library, Cole detected something she'd never made him privy to. Something like vulnerability. It unnerved him.

The tears were dribbling out of her best friend, Andrea, a perfect specimen of *Homo dramaticus* and known to be mortally in touch with her emotions. Cole had no desire to get drawn into her theatrics and was half a step away when he distinctly heard Winnie murmur his name.

She's talking about me? She's talking about me!

He strained to listen but caught only snippets from Andrea's half of the conversation. ". . . you don't know how it feels . . ." ". . . can't let anyone find out . . ." ". . . especially Cole . . ."

Cole examined the evidence: tears, and a vow to keep something secret from him. Together the pieces could form only one picture.

Andrea was secretly in love with him.

Gross.

And absurd. Andrea hated Cole, and the feeling was mutual. This was not Hollywood hate, the obvious kind that meant they were fated to fall for each other. It was the real deal. Besides, among the few assumptions Cole felt reasonably confident making about girls was the hunch that one would never, ever express interest in her best friend's ex.

Cole sidled closer to the stack, squelching the misgiving that there was anything wrong with soaking up a private conversation. If they didn't want to be overheard, they'd text.

Suddenly a voice broke open the vacuum-sealed library air behind him. *"Magst du Goethe?"* Cole fell forward, startled, groping at the books before him for balance, only to shove them flapping through the stack right at Andrea's and Winnie's feet. They locked eyes on him through the gap. Cole caught sight of himself in their expressions and cringed: a perv in training. Andrea hurtled off, wailing. Winnie picked up a fallen book, glanced at the title and back at Cole, eyebrows in attack formation.

"German poetry, Cole? Really?"

Cole scrambled in vain for a response but the answer came from elsewhere. *"Ja, danke,"* said the owner of the voice that sent him sprawling in the first place. A dark-haired girl was reaching through the gap to pluck the book from Winnie's grasp. *"Deutsch Poesie ist mein Favorit. Und Sie?"* Winnie merely puffed out a breath and walked away.

Cole blinked. The girl before him wore red-and-white-striped knee-high socks, a black skirt, and a yellow cardigan over a shirt that ruffled limply at the neck. Her face was winged with dark eye shadow and her was hair pulled into two uneven rubber-banded pigtails. The overall effect was positively Dr. Seussian. On whether this particular instance was heartwarming Seussian or creepy Seussian, he was undecided. Then she spoke again.

"Ich mag Faust. Eine Legende über Satan."

Creepy Seussian. Definitely.

"Sorry," Cole said, backing away slowly. "All I caught was 'Satan.'"

He pivoted and took off, leaving Cindy Lou Who-the-Heck-Is-She to *gesundheit* by herself.

Winnie had vanished. The bell rang and Cole returned to the study carrel for his things only to find Josh and Scott waiting for him. Cole took care to avoid eye contact, remembering a nature program in which a field biologist urged the audience to never, ever look a primate in the peepers.

"Something I can do for you guys?" Cole asked in what he hoped was a casual, carefree tone.

"Did I or did I not tell you to stay away from Winnie?" asked Josh.

Cole remembered advising Gavin not to provoke Josh. He also remembered Gavin saying he had to, because Cole didn't have the nerve to do it himself. Cole suited up. "You did not. You told me to keep my hands off your stuff. Is that what Winnie is to you? Stuff?"

Josh's nostrils flared and he swung tentatively at Cole's books, as though to send them spilling to the floor. But he lacked commitment; the pile only moved a couple of inches toward the lip of the table. He was miscast in the role of Bully.

"Do you want to give it a second try?" Cole offered.

Josh may have still been learning how to throw his weight around, but Scott was a master, and eager to set an example. "You know that jerky little kid in everybody's family?" Scott asked. "The loud cousin who comes over to your house on holidays and gets his cruddy fingerprints on your comics and breaks your PS3 before he's even walked in the door?"

Cole could feel a fight-or-flight decision swiftly approaching. He looked for the door.

"Then he sees your dog. And all the pooch wants to do is sleep. But this kid won't let him, chases him all over the house. And your dog knows he's just a kid. But there's only so much crap he can take from a snot-nosed brat who wants to ride him like he's a horse. So you warn him. You tell him to leave the dog alone. How would he like it if you pulled his tail? But this kid doesn't listen. So when the dog finally sinks his teeth into the little bugger's apple cheeks, part of you feels sorry for him 'cause he's gonna have that scar for the rest of his life. But the rest of you is glad. He deserved what he got." Scott swept the table clean. "You're that little kid, Cole. Only nobody's gonna feel sorry for you when you get your face bit off."

This was the moment to back down. But could Cole live with himself if he did? And, perhaps more importantly, would Winnie ever fall for an invertebrate? "I'm confused. In this scenario is Josh the mutt? Or Winnie?"

Josh leaned in close. "Don't talk about her like that. Don't even think about her. She doesn't think about you."

"The bell rang, guys." The gentle reminder came from Mr. Chetley, the assistant soccer coach and rookie Web design teacher. No one moved. "Is there a problem?"

"No problem, Mr. Chetley," said Josh, secure that Cole had received the message.

"Josh B'Gosh, my dad is Mr. Chetley," said the teacher in his bouncing Southern California accent. "Call me 'Chetley.' Or even 'Chet.' It's all good! What happened with the books, Cola?"

"Cole's just clumsy," said Josh. He and Scott left, Chetley hounding them as they retrieved their things from the computer they'd been using and all the way out the door with an invitation to join his Protest Club. Gavin was president and so far the organization had yet to protest anything save the administration's rules against protest.

Cole gathered his littered books, aware that he'd pay for getting little work done this afternoon by staying up late and losing sleep tonight. He didn't care. He was thinking about Winnie. She had to think about him sometimes. There had to be a way to remind her that she cared about him the way he cared about her. Maybe the key was to make her think less about Josh, or to think less of him. What would it take to open her eyes?

Cole was on his way out when he caught sight of the computer over which Josh and Scott had roosted. An idea took shape.

Cole launched the computer's search engine and examined its recent history. Josh hadn't emptied the cache. The most recent page was a Wikipedia entry. The subject: American serial killers. It took him just a moment to find what he was looking for.

> Perhaps most striking is that when selecting victims, Americans tend to adhere to far more rigid criteria than their worldwide counterparts. An American serial killer knows his victim; an international serial killer discovers his victim.

Gavin was right. There in black-and-white pixels was proof of Josh's cheating. Cole Control-P'd the page, as well as a dozen of the most recent websites Josh and Scott had visited. With every hot, laser-printed sheet of paper, Cole's heart beat a little faster and his grin burned a little brighter. This was the way to get Winnie back where she belonged — with him. He left with the swagger of a private citizen carrying a concealed firearm. He had the gun and the bullet to put an end to Josh and Winnie's relationship. All he had to do now was aim and pull the trigger.

CHAPTER 3

PainAuChoCOLEat: You there?

ShesGottaGavlt: regrettably

PainAuChoCOLEat: We need to talk.

PainAuChoCOLEat: Come over.

ShesGottaGavlt: cant

ShesGottaGavlt: busy

PainAuChoCOLEat: Too busy to punctuate?

ShesGottaGavlt: punctuation is for sheep

ShesGottaGavlt: in my world the semicolon has slaughtered the commas and periods which is why this sentence might be hard to read

PainAuChoCOLEat: Never mind.

ShesGottaGavlt: sup

PainAuChoCOLEat: Remember in middle school when Lauren Schoenmaker was always whispering to her friends and pointing at you and giggling?

PainAuChoCOLEat: And how we thought she was making fun of you?

ShesGottaGavlt: and i retaliated by spiking her hand lotion with numbing cream

ShesGottaGavlt: haha

ShesGottaGavlt: she couldnt feel her fingers all day

ShesGottaGavlt: she walked around like an old timey mummy

ShesGottaGavIt: and had to be hand fed

PainAuChoCOLEat: Is that something you're proud of?

ShesGottaGavIt: it was my finest hour

PainAuChoCOLEat: So you don't regret getting revenge on her?

PainAuChoCOLEat: Even after we found out she was acting that way because she liked you?

ShesGottaGavIt: girls come and go

PainAuChoCOLEat: Uhhh.

PainAuChoCOLEat: Regarding girls —

PainAuChoCOLEat: Specifically, my girl —

PainAuChoCOLEat: And the tool with whom she's run off —

PainAuChoCOLEat: Could be you were right about Josh.

PainAuChoCOLEat: I think he lifted his essay from Wikipedia.

PainAuChoCOLEat: So the question is . . .

PainAuChoCOLEat: Do I pull a Gavin?

ShesGottaGavIt: the answer is

ShesGottaGavIt: duh

WinWin: Hi

PainAuChoCOLEat: No way!

ShesGottaGavIt: yes way

PainAuChoCOLEat: That's not what I meant.

PainAuChoCOLEat: Winnie is IMing.

WinWin: Hello?

ShesGottaGavlt: STEP AWAY FROM THE KEYBOARD

WinWin: Are you ignoring me now?

ShesGottaGavlt: sit tight
ShesGottaGavlt: im coming over
ShesGottaGavlt: ill save you
ShesGottaGavlt: BLOCK HER
ShesGottaGavlt: better idea
ShesGottaGavlt: SIGN OFF

PainAuChoCOLEat: Hi.
<ShesGottaGavlt signed off>
PainAuChoCOLEat: Sorry.
PainAuChoCOLEat: Wasn't at my desk.
WinWin: Let me guess
WinWin: You were baking up a storm
PainAuChoCOLEat: Ha.
PainAuChoCOLEat: No.
PainAuChoCOLEat: (later)
WinWin: Do you make those special Rice Krispies
Treats anymore? The kind with the toffee and the
cinnamon?
PainAuChoCOLEat: You remember them?
WinWin: They were/are my favorite
PainAuChoCOLEat: I do have some marshmallows
lying around.
PainAuChoCOLEat: Maybe I'll break out the
breakfast cereal.
WinWin: You'll never change

PainAuChoCOLEat: I guess that makes one of us.

PainAuChoCOLEat: So . . .

WinWin: So

WinWin: German

PainAuChoCOLEat: Huh?

WinWin: You're piling on the language credits

WinWin: Not a bad idea

WinWin: But you should take something else

WinWin: Only malcontents and medievalists take German

WinWin: Like that weird girl

WinWin: You should take Mandarin

WinWin: Or Arabic

WinWin: Like me

WinWin: Still there?

PainAuChoCOLEat: Thank you for the advice.

PainAuChoCOLEat: I think I'll stick with my plan.

PainAuChoCOLEat: Did you just want to give me an update?

WinWin: I wanted to talk to you about what happened today

WinWin: I didn't mean to be weird

PainAuChoCOLEat: How were you weird?

WinWin: When I saw you at the library

WinWin: Andrea's going through a lot right now

PainAuChoCOLEat: Bad hair day?

WinWin: Her dad died

PainAuChoCOLEat: Oh man.

WinWin: You didn't know? It was all over the news.

PainAuChoCOLEat: I had no idea. What happened?

WinWin: Some kind of freak accident

WinWin: It sucks

PainAuChoCOLEat: I'm sure you're helping a lot.

WinWin: It would be easier to be there for her
if I didn't have to worry about you and Gavin
hassling Josh

WinWin: Maybe you two can lay off him

PainAuChoCOLEat: I didn't realize we were laying
on Josh in the first place.

WinWin: You know what I mean

PainAuChoCOLEat: Actually I don't. He's the one
who got up in Gavin's face after Drick's class. And
then again when he and Scott threatened me in the
library.

WinWin: He told me you threatened him

PainAuChoCOLEat: If you believe that, then you
were wrong and I really have changed.

PainAuChoCOLEat: And you might want to rethink
Harvard/Yale/Princeton/all Ivies/wannabe Ivies/
college in general.

PainAuChoCOLEat: Because Josh has dumbed you
down.

WinWin: I don't know what to say.

PainAuChoCOLEat: You might start with "sorry."

<PainAuChoCOLEat signed off>

A door slammed somewhere below, followed immediately
by his parents' shouts and the rumble of footsteps on stairs.
Gavin crashed in, red in the face and sucking wind.

"I am here . . . to save you . . . from humil . . . iating . . . yourself. . . ."

"Too late," said Cole. He pointed Gavin to the IM on his computer. Gavin looked over Cole's shoulder as he skimmed the conversation.

"Seems pretty clear to me," Gavin said as he flopped onto the bed, "and last week my lit teacher asked me if English is my second language. Winnie is over you."

"But it's obvious Josh lied to her about what happened in the library after she and Andrea took off. She's totally going to check him on that. Plus, what if she finds out he's a cheater! She couldn't afford to be associated with him, because what if people start wondering if she's a cheater, too, like you said?"

"And then what?" Gavin asked. "She comes crawling back to you, begging your forgiveness?"

"I think part of her already wants to come back to me," Cole said with mounting excitement. "See here, where she talks about my baking? Doesn't that mean she's interested and she still thinks about me?"

Gavin was examining the Wikipedia pages Cole had brought home from the library. "All she cares about is getting you to leave her crybaby boyfriend alone. Which you should not do," he added, waving the trove. "Because you can use this stuff to bury him. It proves he lifted half his essay right off of Wikipedia. And we both know how Drick feels about shortcuts."

Lore had it their history teacher had led an unsuccessful attempt to reinstate corporal punishment to the array of faculty powers. It was said he kept a paddle in his office.

Cole bit his fingernail. The thought was tantalizing, for sure.

But he didn't think he was the man for the job. "Drick will figure it out eventually. Won't he?"

Gavin scoffed. "Drick grades by taper light and calculates his bills with an abacus. Do you really think he can operate plagiarism-checking software? Josh would never try this with another teacher because another teacher would catch on, but not Drick. You have to bring it to his attention, and you have to do it with sirens and strobe lights."

"If you think I'm going to rat on him, forget it. The soccer boosters would bury me in balls. And Winnie would never forgive me. As long as they're together, an embarrassment to Josh is an embarrassment to her." Cole braced himself. He knew that if he spoke his mind now, he could never unspeak it. Gavin wouldn't let him. "But I might know another way."

Gavin was intrigued. "Let's hear it."

"Look at this page I printed out. It lists all the Wikipedia RSS feeds Josh subscribes to. He's a thorough little copycat. He wants his work to be up-to-date with all the latest information on crazy killers. With this setup he gets an e-mail every time somebody uploads a change to the entry. Well, in two days he'll be giving his oral report. Why not make sure he delivers the most current information?"

"You want to set a trap?"

"It'd be a trap of his own making. All we have to do is supply him with some fool's-gold facts to copy and paste into his report and let him hang himself."

Gavin had to give Cole his due. "It's a tidy plan."

Cole hesitated. "It isn't too drastic? I keep thinking I should just let it go." Gavin rolled his eyes. "Besides, Winnie asked me to keep the peace for Andrea's sake." Cole began to deliver the news about her father's death, but Gavin cut him off.

"Have you been living under a cookie sheet? Her dad the weatherman died a month ago. He got flamed on Wikipedia and had a nervous breakdown on live TV. Then out of nowhere he got his head caved in by a falling light or something. Andrea will get over it. She's already Tweeting about going to the winter formal."

"You follow Andrea?"

"Hate follow. Look at this." Gavin displayed her Tweet on his phone.

> **Andrea Henderson** @hendersdaughter
> @WinWin100 @OTruffleShuffle: Got my ticket to the formal! Cant wait 2 go w u!

"Sounds pretty grief-stricken to me," said Gavin. "Though I could see her being moved to tears if she was forced to share a table with Winnie's former ex-turned-soon-to-be-current boyfriend, one Mr. Cole Redeker. Think about it." Cole did. "How long will it take Winnie to drop Josh and come running back to you once she finds out she's linked to a cheater?" Now he had Cole's attention. "Quicker than I can finish this sente —"

CHAPTER 4

*T*he day of oral reports rolled around. Cole and Gavin arrived ready to score mucho class-participation points with tons of questions designed solely for Josh.

Cole prepared a little something extra, too.

Class trickled in to receive his signature tomb-sized, toffee-and-cinnamon Rice Krispies Treat. Normally Cole got a buzz from the licking of fingers and the unfolding of wet naps. But today he only cared what Winnie thought.

"What's this?" she asked when he offered one up. As if she didn't know. The treat before her was a yellow Lab puppy, and her eyes screamed, *Please can I pet it?* Cole thrilled to her dawning smile.

"Just a little something to nibble on. Threw together a batch last night."

"Wow."

"It's nothing, really." *Poker face, don't fail me now,* Cole prayed. It wouldn't do to let her see how just how much power she still had over him. Not yet, at least.

"I mean, wow, you're talking to me."

Did she feel guilty? "I wouldn't know how to stay mad at you." Winnie looked away, though there was nothing to look at. "Here. Have a taste."

She lifted the sticky slab to her nose and sniffed. "Did you do something different this time?"

"Same as I always make 'em." Cole saw Josh enter over her shoulder. "You've just been missing out. Josh doesn't cook for you, does he? Exactly what does he do for you?"

If Winnie had an answer to that, she was unable to utter it. Her mouth was webbed shut with marshmallow goo.

"Hey," said Josh, molars grinding. "What's going on?"

"I figured we'd break bread and put all the ugliness of the past behind us."

Josh drew Winnie under his arm. "She's being polite. The second you turn around she'll spit it out. She's on a diet for Sectionals." Winnie blinked.

"I didn't know you were watching Winnie's weight." By the look of growing fury on her face, neither did she.

"I'm only watching out for her." Josh faltered. "If she makes it to States, it'll help her bid for Harvard."

"She'll make it to States with or without a Rice Krispies Treat," Cole said, her most loyal cheerleader. One time he even got ejected from a match for his overzealous support ("Ace her face, Hoffman!" he'd cry). She'd won that tournament in record time.

"I know she'll make it to States," Josh said. "Right, Winnie? Tell him you know I'm just trying to help! It doesn't bother me how fat you get!" Winnie shrugged out of his grip and told Gavin to catch before flipping him the rest of her RKT. Too slow, it smacked against the back of his head and remained there, glued. He was sure to thank Winnie, anyway. But she was already in her seat, shutting down Josh's attempt to apologize.

Drick doddered to the lectern and called for a volunteer to begin. Cole raised his hand. The class let out a sigh. For past reports he'd gone all out, firing up PowerPoint, initiating a role-play, or conducting a Q&A with the town comptroller. But today there was no flash, no bam, no thank-you-ma'am. Today he was lowering the bar — the better to clothesline Josh.

He'd called Gavin the night before, concerned that their plan wouldn't work. "What if Josh doesn't take the bait?" Gavin thought it improbable but suggested a way to whittle down the odds. "You have to tank your report. Watch Josh get cocky and drop his guard. He'll jump at the chance to show you up in front of Winnie." Cole knew his grade could take a slight hit in the process — and a slight hit was all Winnie might need to pull even with him in the race for valedictorian — but the thought of cutting Josh off at the shin guards was worth it.

"The Algonquin Round Table was an American salon," he mumbled. Josh, Winnie, and the rest of his competition leaned forward, waiting for the razzle-dazzle sure to come. "It was filled with witty writers. Their work influenced American letters for decades." Drick expected more from his honors students, and everyone expected more from Cole. His deliberately botched delivery had provided an opening for his enemies.

Ten minutes later, Cole finished and looked up. His classmates were slack-jawed and cross-eyed, where their eyes were open at all.

"Thank you for that roller-coaster ride, Mr. Redeker," Drick quacked sarcastically. "However, your speech-giving does not quite rise to the level of your cooking." Gavin's laugh clanked from the back of the class. "Who would care to follow up? Is anyone left awake?"

Several hands shot into the air. Josh's was the first among them. He sauntered to the lectern with a box under his arm and addressed his classmates with the exceptional confidence of one who dared wear cargo shorts on the eve of winter.

"A history of serial killers," he announced. "Check it out. H. H. Holmes, America's first documented serial killer, was arrested in 1894. By the time of his execution, he'd confessed to twenty-seven murders, but may have committed as many as two hundred, and had set the bar for a cavalcade of killers to come. Here are but a few. . . ."

What Josh lacked in imagination he made up for with gusto. Nobody was in danger of falling asleep by the time he concluded his speech, taking the class on a tour of American serial killers throughout the years. Josh had a flair for describing the evolution of murder technique, as well as props for emphasis. With each case study he removed from his box an ordinary household item — a melon baller, an air pump, a tea cozy — and demonstrated how a maniac twisted its purpose from helpful to harmful.

"So as the now-deceased killer Frank N. Berry might say, paper beats rock, and rock beats scissors, but coffee grinder beats bone."

"An exhaustive exploration of human depravity." Drick shuddered as his students attempted to settle their stomachs, lacquered with Rice Krispies Treats. "Marvelous job. Are there questions for Mr. Truffle?" Cole caught a look from Gavin. *What are you waiting for?* it harped.

"I have a question," he blurted. This was it. Success or failure — and quite possibly Josh's future, not to mention Cole's future with Winnie — hinged on this moment.

"I feel like every time the police identify another serial killer it becomes national news. But I've never heard of this Frank N. Berry until now."

"I'm not surprised," yawned Mr. Expert. "It's an obscure case, but a fascinating one. Berry was called the Rise-and-Dine Killer. He'd surprise his victims in their homes, early in the day, and always sitting at the breakfast table."

"That's weird," supplied Gavin. "You'd think that would be a hard time to catch a person unawares, not to mention get away unseen."

"That's not the strangest thing by far." Josh was in his element. "Berry himself was murdered before he could be brought to justice. And that wasn't some random killing, either."

"Wait a second," said Cole. "Are you suggesting the serial killer was killed by a serial killer?"

"That's Horatio Crunch's theory," said Josh. "He was a former police captain, best known for nabbing the notorious child murderer Trixie R. Abbot and recently went on record saying he believes the person who killed Berry is also responsible for the murders of several other people all over the country. Some say the Cap'n was close to catching Berry's killer, too — before he also got iced."

"Wait, someone murdered the Cap'n, too?" asked Andrea, appalled.

Josh nodded, enjoying his turn as teacher. "But no one knows who. Maybe the FBI does. Maybe they don't. Maybe they're just trying to avoid starting a panic. Right now they aren't talking."

"Duh, it was the same dude who did Berry! He knew Crunch was getting too close!"

"Has this mystery killer a modus operandi?" asked Drick.

Josh lowered his voice, crypt quiet. "Autopsies have revealed that both Berry and Crunch died from an injection of a highly concentrated dose of a designer drug called Mendacido."

Gavin inquired as to whether he could get that over the counter or did he need a prescription?

"You'd probably have an easier time getting it from a dealer," answered Josh. "Its street name is Sugar Shock. The facts of this case are limited, and what precious little the authorities do know just begs more questions. For instance, why does the killer slather his — or her — victims in sweet golden-brown honey, fresh from the comb?"

"Lemme get this straight," said Cole. "You're saying these people basically OD'd on sugar and were found coated in honey?"

"Head to toe. And not sugar — Sugar *Shock*," Josh corrected. "That's how this killer got his name. The Cap'n dubbed him . . . the Sugar Bear."

This name of evil passed over the class like the shadow of a great and ravenous man-eating bird. For a moment, no one spoke. No one moved. No one breathed. Then Cole rolled his eyes. "Ha-ha, Josh. Joke's over. Be real now."

"It is real."

"You expect us to believe that?"

Winnie swung her head around, her hair slashing the face of the student behind her. "What is your problem, Cole?" Cole steeled himself. He knew when he signed on to Gavin's plan that Winnie might take up arms against him.

"It's all right," Josh told her. "I'm happy to address Cole's concerns. I've done my research."

"I'd be curious to know where you're getting your facts. From the back of a cereal box?"

"That's quite enough, Mr. Redeker. One does not impugn a classmate's work without good reason."

Winnie dialed up a death stare. "I can think of a reason," she said, "but it isn't good."

There was no backing out now. Cole forged ahead, and hoped she'd thank him later. "The reason lines every breakfast aisle in America. Am I seriously the only person to pick up on the fact that 'Sugar Bear' is the cartoon face of Golden Crisp? The wholesome honey-sweetened puffed-wheat cereal?"

Josh drew breath to respond but failed to follow through, unsure. Winnie spoke up in his defense. "That could be a break in the case! Maybe the Sugar Bear is an unhinged employee of Post Cereals!"

Giggles spread across the room at the speed of gossip. Josh couldn't shut them down fast enough. "This has to be a coincidence!"

Drick crossed his arms as he gazed reproachfully at Josh, who was red as a rose. Not coincidentally, Winnie was the same color. Cole yearned to comfort her.

"You have to believe me, Mr. Drick," Josh pleaded. "I swear, this is the truth!"

"The truth about *cereal* killers, maybe," said Cole. "But not about *serial* killers."

"I didn't make this up," Josh whined. "I got it straight from —"

He had just enough smarts to stop that sentence before he finished, but not enough never to have begun it at all.

"I believe you were about to cite your sources, Mr. Truffle?"

Josh looked to Winnie, desperate for help, but he was on his own. The only thing left to do was confess.

"Wikipedia," he said, head hung low.

Drick squeezed the bridge of his nose between his thumb and forefinger, and spent the remainder of the period lecturing the class on the limits of the Internet as a research tool. Josh stood there the whole time, up to his knees in shame, his head and hands locked in an invisible stockade. But that's what Cole wanted. Wasn't it?

Drick still wasn't finished when the bell mercifully rang. Winnie scooped up her things and rushed out. Cole couldn't catch up to her, caught in the glut of classmates knotted in the door. Josh stayed behind for a private chat with their teacher. Drick was interested to know what role Wikipedia may have played in the work Josh had submitted earlier in the semester. From the look on Josh's face it was apparent he knew the conversation would be a long one.

Gavin was disappointed the paddle hadn't made an appearance, but otherwise deemed the class a resounding success. "I love it when a plan comes together," he murmured. Cole might have loved it, too, if he hadn't then spotted Winnie. Andrea's hand was on her shoulder, which jerked irregularly, in time with her wet gasps. A strange sound came from Winnie's lips, strange but familiar. He'd heard this sound before, but never from her.

Not choking. Crying.

CHAPTER 5

*G*avin presided over the remnants of a pizza, a murder scene of tomato sauce and cheese. "Sure you don't want more? Last slice, up for grabs."

Cole shook his head. They were toasting Josh's ruin in their usual hangout, the prime booth at Benito's, a grimy, beloved pizza joint situated at the top of a hill overlooking the high school. A greasy piece of paper had been taped above the table for three years. Written on it in Benito's old-man scrawl was *IF YOUR NAME ISN'T COLE YOU DON'T SIT HERE.* Cole had been awarded the honor for single-handedly saving the neighborhood institution when a gourmet sandwich shop moved in next door and began siphoning off the post-school crowd with free Wi-Fi and bottomless coffee. Cole's recipe for a new and improved crust shuttered the competition. The space next door to Benito's had been empty ever since.

"More for me," said Gavin. "Don't let Benito see you turn up your nose at his pie. He'll be crushed. Benito *finito.*"

Cole rested his forehead to the table. "I'm not hungry. My appetite was washed away by Winnie's tears."

"If someone dear to your heart, say, yours truly, had been unmasked as a total phony, you'd cry, too."

"But I made her cry!"

"Good for you. You're well on your way to liberating her from Josh."

"I'd never have gone ahead with it if I'd known I'd reduce her to a puddle of goo in the process."

"Girls cry," said Gavin. "That's what they do."

"When they see *you* coming."

"Those are tears of joy, similar to the ones you may shed when Winnie begs you to take her back."

Cole tried to imagine that scenario, but saw only the moment after Drick's class when Andrea guided Winnie down the hall, her eyes stinging and half blind. The sequence was on auto-repeat, and his heart belly flopped with each replay.

"And she will want you back," Gavin soothed with a pat to Cole's head. "But first she has to bring herself to admit she made a mistake dropping you for that clod. Clearly that may take more than one prank."

The bell above the door jingled. Mr. Chetley entered in a tracksuit and sweat bands, a walking ad for American Apparel. The young teacher scanned the room for a seat — or a friend — and found only Cole and Gavin's banquet. "Crud," groaned Gavin. "He's probably wondering why I quit Protest Club."

"Why did you quit Protest Club?"

"I decided I like things the way they are. Quick, look busy." Too late. Chetley was upon them.

"Hey, Cola. Gavver. Mind if I join you?" He didn't wait for an answer, sliding in. "I'm famished. Just came from the game. Didn't see you guys there."

"We prefer to support the team from a distance," said Gavin, "lest our stardom distract from the action on the field."

"Next time don't be so shy. We can use all the friendly faces we can muster."

"Tough game?" asked Gavin.

"We got slaughtered."

Cole perked up. The varsity soccer squad had been touted to go undefeated this year, largely on Josh's prowess on center forward. "Josh must be heartbroken," he fished.

"I'm sure he is. Especially since he got pulled from the game. . . ."

Cole and Gavin looked at each other.

"Scott stepped up to take his place but he just doesn't have Josh's imagination. He's not *one* with the ball."

"If Josh is so vital, why didn't he play? Did he get hurt?"

Chetley glanced around. "I'm not supposed to talk about it," he said, desperate to talk about it. "But you guys are cool. Coach got a call from the athletic director at halftime. Josh's on academic probation. He's on water boy duty until the heat dies down."

Cole felt Gavin's swift kick under the table. His stomach folded and unfolded. Was that the return of his appetite, or the power of guilt? "No kidding. Academic probation?"

"I'm as surprised as you are," Chetley lamented. "I know I'm new here but I like to think I'm a pretty good judge of character. Josh seemed like a stand-up guy."

"It's sad when our heroes let us down." Gavin could barely contain his glee.

Chetley sighed. "I guess that's why he could barely look at his girlfriend."

Cole slowed up. "What happened with Josh and Winnie?"

"Is that her name?" Chetley hooked a string of mozzarella from the dregs around his finger. "I've seen her at the games. She and Josh seem pretty tight . . ."

A montage zipped through Cole's head. Every held hand

between Winnie and Josh that he'd been unfortunate enough to witness.

". . . when he's not giving her the brush-off. He left once he got the word he wouldn't play. Marched right by her and wouldn't stop, even as she called his name."

Cole was grateful for the intelligence, but creeped out by its source, and quickly made his exit.

The wind was picking up in the parking lot. Cole gazed down the hill to the high school. The soccer field was empty but the lights were on in the tennis bubble. Winnie would be at practice. The bond between Josh and Winnie was eroding. Maybe this was Cole's chance to pry them apart. As he loped down the hill away from Benito's, he set aside the thought that if he got his way, his hands would be dirty.

Someone watched Cole from the shadows. Someone with a plan. And if that plan came to pass, Cole's hands wouldn't just be dirty.

They'd be bloody, too.

CHAPTER 6

Cole shouldered open the heavy door to the tennis bubble and sucked up a lungful of hard-court air. The scent of vulcanized rubber and bleachers conjured memories of cheering Winnie on as she lobbed serves at dopey-eyed foes.

Then another thing occurred to him: eighty miles per hour of felt to the face.

The hurtling tennis ball caught Cole dead between the eyes. His head snapped backward and the lights above swam and then drowned in darkness.

He stirred moments later. The pain bubbling from his nose took a backseat to the position in which he found himself: flat on his back, his head nestled on something pillowy and warm. Legs. A lap. A girl's lap.

Two voices cut through the murk. He recognized one, though he couldn't place it. The other he knew right away. He opened his eyes a squint, enough to see, leaning above him, silhouetted by the lights and a scrim of hair. . . .

"Winnie?"

"Nein, nicht Winnie," came the voice above him, calm and gibberishy and *not* Winnie. Her dark hair and eyes were offset with a mod white terry cloth headband. She may have lacked the distinctive makeup, but there was no mistaking the girl from his library encounter a few days before. *"Ich bin Lila."* She

tapped her sternum. A tennis bracelet of skulls wriggled on her wrist. *"Lila. Bist du verletzt? Wie viele finger siehst du?"*

"He doesn't speak German." *That* was Winnie.

"Try Loser-as-a-Second-Language," came a third voice. "He's fluent." And *that* was Andrea. Cole lifted his head and focused. Andrea was bouncing a ball with her racket in time with the pounding in his head. Winnie stood nearby at his feet, close enough to care but not enough to touch.

"Are you okay?" asked Winnie.

He tested a fingertip to his nose. The pain was dizzying, but there was no blood. Then why was his face wet?

"That's drool," Andrea supplied.

"What happened?"

Andrea answered for Winnie, as if she didn't trust her best friend to stick to her talking points. "You got aced. The *fräulein* here was trying out for the team and you bumbled right into the path of her serve."

The girl cradling Cole's head looked back down at him with concern, fanning several fingers in his face.

"Wie viele Finger ich halten up?"

Cole's eyes throbbed with each bounce of the ball. "Does anyone understand what she's saying?" he moaned.

Winnie snatched the ball from Andrea. "Say 'three,' Cole."

"Three?"

"Hooray, he can still count," griped Andrea, hustling Winnie away.

"Wait!" Cole tried to lurch to a seated position only to swoon back into Lila's arms. "Please. I need to talk to you." Winnie pulled away from Andrea and faced him. Her shoulders rose and fell visibly with each breath, a sure sign that his time was limited.

"Talk."

Here's your opening, Cole. Don't muck it up now. "How do I look?" *Smooth.*

Andrea leaned in. "She's not your mirror, Cole."

Winnie stayed Andrea with a hand. "Like you could have a broken nose and are in need of medical attention."

Beneath him, Cole felt German girl/Lila/tennis assassin twinge.

"Feels swollen, is all. It's not that bad."

"I'd call it a vast improvement," offered Andrea, eyes on her phone.

Cole ignored her, focusing on Winnie. But her gaze skittered.

"Put some ice on it," Winnie advised. "Lots. Is that it?"

Cole wondered the same thing.

They'd been allies. Confidants. Pals. Now he lay before her, concussed, and the best she could muster was a suggestion that he pack his snotty nose with ice.

"I came to see how you were doing. I saw you in the hall after Drick's class. I was . . ." *Useless. Unworthy. Distraught.* ". . . worried. I've never seen you like that. I hated it."

Winnie's expression seemed to soften. There, in the bite of her lip, was the seed of a connection.

"And then I heard you and Josh had some kind of fight at his soccer game."

Winnie bit down harder. A good sign. Andrea broke off from her texting. A bad sign.

"You don't miss much, do you, Cole?" Andrea said, looking up from her phone. "Probably because your beady little eyes are never off Winnie for long." Cole left for dead any notion he ever had that Andrea harbored an interest in him. "You spend your days watching and waiting for Josh to slip up so you can swoop in."

Suddenly Cole felt stripped to his least dignified underwear: tighty-whities, the underwear left over when everything else had already been worn twice, the underwear of last resort. "I don't know what you're talking about."

"Please. You're so obvious, Cole. You came here to give Winnie a shoulder to cry on, hoping she'd pour out her heart about Josh and realize what a prince you look like in comparison. You think she deserves better. A poet. A disciple. A personal chef. You."

"Ich möchte jemanden, der für mich backen," said Lila in a scrambled alphabet.

"No one's talking to you, Brunhilda."

"Is she right, Cole?" asked Winnie.

Yes, but . . . "No," replied Cole. "I'm a terrible poet."

Winnie didn't laugh. Instead, she closed her eyes. When she opened them a moment later, it was all over. "I have to go. I'm late meeting Josh."

"You remember Josh," said Andrea. "Her boyfriend?"

The word fell on Cole like a sandbag. "Don't you mean her ex-boyfriend?" He looked at Winnie. "The one you broke up with because he copies his work straight off of the Internet and can't tell Hannibal Lecter from Count Chocula? The ex-boyfriend who was dragging you down?"

Winnie's jaw tightened. "No, she meant my boyfriend. The one I did not break up with just because he's under all kinds of pressure with soccer and class and college applications, and let

Scott convince him to take a stupid shortcut. The boyfriend I am still with because he doesn't cling to me or crowd me or make it impossible for me to be anything other than perfect. I mean my boyfriend. Not my ex-boyfriend. Not you. You and I are not getting back together. Ever."

She and Andrea departed, leaving Cole alone, with his wounded pride thudding in his gut. And Lila. He wriggled from her clutches.

"Es tut mir leid," she said as he wobbled to his feet, grabbing the ball. *"Sie ist nicht würdig."* Cole needed no translator to tell him what she'd said. The meaning was clear by the quality of her tone: serrated. "I agree," he breathed, wandering out.

Lila watched him go, then said aloud to herself, *"Keine Sorge,* Cole. She'll regret it."

CHAPTER 7

Cole placed an empty cardboard box beside his bed and faced his desk. One by one, he removed all things Winnie.

First date. Dinner at the Golden Phoenix. Pan-seared jade dumplings. Abalone lotus. Mexican Coke. Tacked to his bulletin board was the scrap of paper he'd unrolled from the fortune cookie they shared.

Fortune Not Found: Abort, Retry, Ignore?

"It's an omen," teased Winnie.

"We have no fortune. We'll make our own," Cole said.

The fortune went into the box.

ShesGottaGavIt: what the dilly

One-month anniversary. Winnie's gift to him. A mix CD. "Forget You," *Glee*-cast version. "Defying Gravity," *Wicked*. "Baby," Justin Bieber. Gavin said it was one Disney Radio single away from a tween top forty. Cole suspected Gavin was right about her taste, so he couldn't tell him about the bonus Miley Cyrus track she'd secretly embedded at the end. Besides. He kinda liked it.

Into the box.

ShesGottaGavIt: you see my chick is one of a kind

ShesGottaGavlt: i know you wish your chick was a
rider like mine
ShesGottaGavlt: when you see my mission know
my shortys a dime
ShesGottaGavlt: what she doing with them chicks
ShesGottaGavlt: she be skipping the line

Yearbook. Page 57, Model UN, Winnie and Cole, elected
co-secretary-generals. Page 63, Winnie and Cole win the super-
lative, "I'm Never Wrong." Inside cover, Winnie's inscription. *I
can't believe it's over!! Next year seniors, then college!! But first,
summer!! Feldman's, fireflies, and goose bumps!* Next to it, Gavin's
inscription. *Ditch Winnie and come with me to the beach!* Winnie
did the ditching.

Tear out the pages, put them in the box.

ShesGottaGavlt: do you not like my busta rhymes

Photo. Winnie, helmeted for a ropes course. Scaling a wall
and looking up into Cole's lens, mouth open in a waving flag
of a grin. Box.

Photo. Prom. How should he stand? Smile with teeth or
without? Where should he put his hands? On her hips, arms
stiff, posed like an action figure lacking elbow joints. Box.

Ticket stubs. Box. Postcards. Box. Invitations. Playbills,
carnival-game prizes, valentines, birthday cards. The leather
bracelet she bought him on a trip to New York. He had to
psych himself up to feel cool enough to wear it. Box.

When he was finished, his desk resembled an archaeologi-
cal dig. Half-emptied drawers, half open. Constellations of

thumbtack holes in his bulletin board where he'd affixed photos. Vast desert spaces on his desktop created by the absence of Winniabilia.

Had he only been Winnie's glorified placeholder? Did she have no one better to hang around with until Josh came along? Was every memory he had of their relationship counterfeit?

Cole's computer dinged again with another message from Gavin.

> ShesGottaGavIt: whenever you feel like
> acknowledging my existence
> PainAuChoCOLEat: I'm here.
> ShesGottaGavIt: let me take you out
> ShesGottaGavIt: to drown your sorrows

Cole looked at the box, at all the mementos he'd purged from his desk. Not one of them was genuine. It wasn't enough that Josh had taken her away. Now they'd taken everything he'd once known to be true, too. It wasn't fair.

> PainAuChoCOLEat: I'm thinking we should drown
> Winnie and Josh instead.
> ShesGottaGavIt: !
> ShesGottaGavIt: See what I did there?
> ShesGottaGavIt: Punctuation!
> ShesGottaGavIt: Capitalization!
> ShesGottaGavIt: You've shocked me into grammar!
> PainAuChoCOLEat: I'm going to get back at them.

> ShesGottaGavIt: Sorry, passed out.

ShesGottaGavIt: Are you for real?

PainAuChoCOLEat: Josh.

PainAuChoCOLEat: Scott.

PainAuChoCOLEat: Andrea.

ShesGottaGavIt: Winnie?

PainAuChoCOLEat: Winnie.

ShesGottaGavIt: I feel like a proud papa.

ShesGottaGavIt: Look at my boy.

ShesGottaGavIt: All grown up.

PainAuChoCOLEat: I want to do to them what they did to me.

ShesGottaGavIt: Turn them into depressive shells of their former selves?

PainAuChoCOLEat: Embarrass them.

PainAuChoCOLEat: Make them hate each other.

PainAuChoCOLEat: Ruin them.

ShesGottaGavIt: And how are you going to do that?

PainAuChoCOLEat: http://en.wikipedia.org/wiki /Josh_Truffle

Gavin clicked the link.

Josh Truffle
From Wikipedia, the free encyclopedia

ShesGottaGavIt: I was unaware Josh had a Wikipedia page.

PainAuChoCOLEat: I got the idea from that story you told me about Andrea's dad. Keep reading.

Josh Truffle (born June 1, 1995) is an American high school student and soccer player for the Springfield High School Raiders of Springfield, Connecticut. He led his section with fifteen goals in 2013, attracting the attention of numerous scouts for Division One college soccer programs. However, Truffle saw his future go down in flames after revelations of systematic cheating in several SHS classes.

It went on, outlining Josh's humiliation in class and on the field. But Cole didn't stop there. He unloaded every detail about how Josh snaked Winnie, and made up a few scuzzier ones, to boot.

> ShesGottaGavIt: I like the part where you have Josh and Winnie running a slave trade out of the locker room.
> PainAuChoCOLEat: I only wrote that to see if you were reading closely.
> PainAuChoCOLEat: So what do you think?
> ShesGottaGavIt: I think it's a step in the right direction.
> ShesGottaGavIt: But if you want real and lasting payback, you need to do more.
> PainAuChoCOLEat: Like what?
> ShesGottaGavIt: Like
> ShesGottaGavIt: Make them hurt each other.
> ShesGottaGavIt: See, if Josh knocked your teeth out, you wouldn't be surprised.
> ShesGottaGavIt: Because he's your enemy.
> ShesGottaGavIt: But if I knocked your teeth out . . .

ShesGottaGavIt: It would come out of left field.

ShesGottaGavIt: Because we're besties.

PainAuChoCOLEat: It would be a betrayal.

ShesGottaGavIt: Unfortunately, that's where my wisdom ends.

ShesGottaGavIt: I don't know how to set one of them against the other.

Cole remembered something Winnie had said in the tennis bubble. It had been Scott's suggestion that Josh turn to Wikipedia to source his work.

PainAuChoCOLEat: Maybe I do.

Gavin came over later and they worked all night fine-tuning Josh's page and constructing four more, one each for Andrea, Scott, Winnie, and Mr. Drick. Gavin argued that Drick deserved the mischief for his habit of capricious grading. By then Cole was feeling just punchy enough to agree.

Shortly before dawn, Cole finally felt ready to deliver their work into the world. "Do you think this will work?"

Gavin cracked his neck. "You'd better hope so, because I don't have the energy to keep hatching revenge plots with you. If this doesn't put them in the ground, you're on your own."

Cole wondered about that as he gave the pages a final once-over. They seemed to be missing something. A final thumbed nose. He had an idea and began to type, revising each page with one or two sentences.

"What are you doing?" asked Gavin.

It was childish. It was spiteful. It was over the top. But it was the finishing touch that made him feel strong, like he'd just rocked twenty pull-ups with ease before his entire gym class. His blood rumbled in his veins like rapids and he took a big, confident, gladiator breath as he presented the final product to Gavin for approval.

"I can't put them in the ground for real," he told Gavin. "But I can do it for fun."

Gavin's eyes gleamed as he drank in Cole's additions: Deaths. For Josh, Scott, Andrea, Drick — and Winnie. Each one tailored to the subject and the wrongs committed. "The student surpasses the master. I didn't know you were so twisted."

Neither did Cole. But the ends of his enemies had come naturally to him. Still, it wasn't like it meant anything. He wanted them to feel pain, but he didn't want anyone dead. This part was just a joke.

Until later that day. When it wasn't.

CHAPTER 8

Cole paused near the entrance to the high school and took in his surroundings. He wanted to remember this moment. A few dried and curling leaves still clung to the oaks guarding the entry. A single frozen crust of snow was pasted to the pavement. It was all that remained of the storm that had crashed through two weeks before. The warm front that had replaced it melted away everything else, including Cole's melancholy. Behind him lay life with Winnie. Before him lay . . . something else. Something good. A renewed focus on academics. Valedictorian. An Ivy. Italian vowels and six figures and the mind-numbing job his parents wanted for him. But he would also have his chef's kitchen. And without fantasies of reuniting with Winnie to distract him, his cooking would get back to form. Maybe the something awaiting wasn't necessarily "good." Maybe it was just "better."

He joined the stream of students filing into the school, prepared to dine on the gossip of Josh and Winnie's undoing.

But there was no feast to be had.

He passed not one, not two, but three cliques devoted to spreading of bad news. Nobody asked him for his ex-boyfriend take on the allegations he had unleashed onto the Internet just hours ago. Something was off.

"Yeah, something's off!" exclaimed Gavin when he found Cole at his locker. "We were too busy crafting their demise to remember to leak the pages! No one's talking about them because no one knows they exist!"

Cole suggested that remedying that wouldn't be too hard, but Gavin warned him not to get cocky. "It's not like one of us can just Tweet it. We have to cover our tracks. The best thing would be for someone else to break the story for us."

Cole spun out his locker combo, thinking. He didn't know such a person. They might have to take their chances, create a fake Facebook profile or something and hope it couldn't be traced —

Something flapped in his face. A sheet of paper taped to the inside of his locker door. Attached to it was a yellow sticky. Neither of them had been put there by Cole.

"What is it?" asked Gavin.

Written on the sticky were the words, *Here's a preview of a story that will hit later today. Hope you like it. Still standing by you. Alles liebe, WW.* The document was a printout of a *Muckraker* article dated today. Cole scanned the piece, headlined "Soccer Stunner." "Looks like someone else beat us to it." Cole lowered his voice and read the article. "I think there is someone who could help us out," he said. "Somebody who owes me one. The same somebody who left this for me to find. Walda Winchell. Writes for the *Muckraker*."

Gavin shook his head. "I don't like it. Everyone knows 'Walda Winchell' is an alias. She could be Gossip Girl for all we know! How can you trust her? She broke into your locker. Besides, she's German. You can't trust a German. They eat *flammekuchen* and *pfannkuchen* by the handful."

"German?" Cole's eyes fell stupidly on the *Alles liebe* written on the sticky. He looked up just in time to catch a glimpse

51

of rainbow tube socks, Birkenstocks, and black hair disappear around a corner. He took off after her, deaf to Gavin calling his name.

The next corridor was empty. The classrooms that lined it were locked, their teachers yet to arrive for first period. There was only one way to go, and Cole launched into it.

The girls' bathroom.

Lila was perched on a sink with her phone, her reflection revealing she was well ahead in a game of *Words with Friends*. Cole stopped in his tracks This was a place in which his kind was not supposed to trespass. Like a fairy fort.

Lila put her phone away. The look on her face was not one of indignation. She looked . . . pleased. Almost tickled. "First time here? Is it all you'd imagined?"

"You speak English."

"Kind of hard not to in America."

"You're also Walda Winchell."

"To my readers," she chirped, extending her hand. "You can call me Lila. Don't worry. I used soap and everything."

Cole shook her hand, warm to the touch.

"You're wondering why I let you think I was German."

"Among other things. Like how you broke into my locker."

"Sorry, trade secret. So are you going to give me your review?"

"Review?" He felt like a racquetball, smashed off her racquet.

"Of my piece. You like the lead? It's fair and balanced? You feel the players are accurately represented?"

"I think it's your finest work yet," he said.

She grinned. "I didn't go after your precious Winnie too hard?"

Then he remembered why he'd followed her inside.

"Like I said. Finest work yet. Except it's incomplete."

No more grin. "Excuse me?"

"There's more to the story. I'd hate for you to release this only to find out you missed the biggest part." He held out his hand for her phone. "May I?"

She turned it over, curious. Cole used the browser to call up Josh's Wikipedia page. "I found it online last night," he said. "I'm surprised no one else has. Read."

It took her all of five seconds to find the part that made her eyes widen.

Cole refreshed the *Muckraker*'s website all day. He was sitting next to Gavin in Chetley's class, working on their Web designs, when the story finally hit. Cole smacked Gavin in the side and nodded at the screen. The story read almost exactly as it had on the hard copy Lila left for him in his locker.

Truffle's future is not the only one left in question. With their star center forward on academic probation, the SHS varsity soccer team is suddenly without their greatest weapon. But according to the Wikipedia page of one teammate, the season is not lost. An examination of Scott Dare's page yields this interesting tidbit: It was at his suggestion that Truffle take the shortcut that ultimately led to his benching. And who has been designated Truffle's replacement at center forward for this all-important moment when college scouts are making their visits?

Scott Dare himself.

More as it develops . . .

Gavin was disappointed. "Walda didn't mention that the Wikipedia profile says he's supposed to die a gruesome death."

Suddenly the door slammed open, gunshot loud. The class jumped as one. Standing and seething in the door was Josh.

"Hey, Josh B'Gosh," said Chetley. "You're early for class. Don't I have you next period?"

Josh ignored him as he stalked up to Scott, whose baseball cap tilted just off-center. He only managed to get one "dude" out of his mouth before Josh filled it with his fist.

Scott was on the floor and smiling blood where Josh had split his lip. Josh leapt on top of him and sank a flurry of punches before Scott could raise his own arms in defense. Cole and Gavin stood with the rest of the class, giving the struggling pair a wide berth as Scott tried to scrabble to his feet. Cole lost sight of them behind a row of desks, but could hear the awful smack of knuckle on skin and wet grunts of both guys as they struggled for control. It took what felt like minutes for Chetley to intervene, and even longer to succeed. His glasses were knocked askew as he thrust himself between the two and pushed Josh back.

"Office! Now!"

Josh's face was scratched on one side as he yelled, tearing the lining from his vocal cords, "He comes, too! He set me up! He's taking my spot on the team!"

Scott was goateed in blood. Cole thought he might be missing a tooth. "What are you talking about?!"

"You wanted me to get caught so I'd get kicked off the team and you could take my spot on the roster!"

Gavin looked at Cole. *Jackpot.*

CHAPTER 9

Everything that happened was Josh's fault, Scott decided. He was the one who'd let his grades slip. He was the one who begged for help. All Scott had done was show his friend how to fluff his grades with a few Internet-related shortcuts. Scott had been getting away with it for years, and Josh could, too — so long as he followed a few simple rules.

Paraphrase. Typos. Get a name wrong here, a date wrong there.

And, above all, settle for a B. Never get greedy for As. But Josh got greedy. And he got caught. Now that he was riding the bench, Scott would play first string. Scott would score the goals. Scott would score the ladies. Scott would be the star.

Dusk was the color of a bruise when Coach blew the final whistle and the guys trudged off to the showers. Scott stayed behind. Up and down the field he dribbled, ironing out the kinks in his footwork. He lined up a row of balls before the goal and punched them in, the net shuddering with every successful shot. There were a lot of successful shots. Good enough to make his case. Good enough to —

Plunge him into the dark. With no warning, the field lights went out.

Scott shut his eyes and opened them. He saw only blackness, and the phosphorescent inkblot wake that bright lights leave in their sudden absence. There was a flutter at the back of his neck. He groped at the bug or the bird or the hand that had brushed him.

Nothing was there. All he felt were his fine, sandy-blond hairs. They stood on end.

Scott waited for his eyes to adjust, remembering the stories his parents liked to tell about his childhood fear of the monsters under the bed. Scott couldn't remember far back enough to know whether those stories were BS, but at least he wasn't afraid of the dark anymore. He was too old for that stuff.

Usually.

Now, alone at night on the broad, flat expanse of the soccer field, the dark did not feel like just the dark. The something else was near, the something other than him. Scott had the sensation of standing on the middle of a wild, frozen lake, and the ice beneath his feet was cracking.

Snap.

Scott jumped. Had he heard something? A twig breaking? Or was it in his head?

Rustle.

He could see a little better now, and made out the white skeleton of the goal. The sound had come from behind it, somewhere in the grove that marked the end of the school's property.

"Hello?"

Scott listened, but heard only the wind through the branches. He walked past the goal, to the edge of the trees, forcing his gait to resemble a stroll. "Hey," he called.

No answer. It was a squirrel. A woods sound. A nothing to worry about.

Smack-whoosh-chunk.

A large and heavy something bashed him, square in the back of the head.

Scott face-planted into the frozen ground. *Now* there was light. Lots of it. The whiteout light of pain. He rolled to his side and whimpered. A loose tooth clinked inside his mouth. *Great.*

Crunch.

Crunch.

Crunch.

Footsteps on the frosty, crystalizing grass. Scott's eyes focused on a soccer ball nearby. Was that what had hit him? Someone was watching from the trees and beaned him when he wasn't looking? Two potshots in one day? Scott got to his hands and knees. Time to clean someone's clock.

Crunch.

Crunch.

The footsteps stopped right above him.

"I am going to destroy you," Scott said, looking up.

Just in time to get stomped on his face.

Then, nothing.

Then, the throb in his head.

Then, eyes open.

He was lying prone in the dark, on a damp, tiled floor.

And he couldn't move.

"Hello?" he called. There was no answer.

Something was husked around him, squeezing his arms against his sides and pressing his legs together, like he was limbless, a fish wrapped in a net.

A net.

A soccer net. Someone had knocked him out and bundled him into a soccer net.

"Okay. Ha-ha. Good joke. You can let me go now." There was only silence.

"Hey, can anyone hear me? I need some help."

No help came.

Scott took a deep breath and flexed every muscle in his body. The nylon net pulled against him, etching its pattern into the flesh of his face, arms, and shins. The net stretched.

Push.

Yes. He could feel it. A hairsbreadth of room between him and his cocoon. If he could make that much room, he could make more. Enough to shimmy his arms up in front of him. Enough to win the use of his fingers. Enough to slip free.

Push harder.

He set his jaw and doubled down, glazed in sweat, arching his back and puffing out his chest.

Push!

The net yawned, expanding and elongating. Just a little more room and he could slide his greasy arm into play.

He didn't have a little more. His muscles gave out and the net reasserted itself, a thousand tiny bungee pythons. Scott shriveled to the cold embrace of the floor, opened his mouth, and screamed into it. He screamed and screamed, screamed until his voice grew ragged.

"This isn't funny!"

He hurt. All over. His arms and legs and hands and knees and skin. The net was wrapped so tightly that every attempt to move was agony. The pain fractured his thoughts like an icebreaker. But one thing was clear.

He had to get out.

Scott took a deep breath and forced up another shout.

No one called. Just a strange *bwop* and the sound of his gasps and the net narrowing against his skin. Something skittered down his temple and across his ear. He yelped and floundered. Was it a cockroach? A spider?

Bwop.

There it was again.

Bwop.

Scott concentrated on the sound. Now it was familiar.

Bwop.

And there was an odor. Chlorine. Metal. Funk. The locker room? It was the team. Some kind of prank. Hazing for the new captain.

"Ha-ha. Come on, guys. Enough already. Joke's over." His voice reverberated off the surfaces around him. There was no other sound, save —

The lights came on, humming and fluorescent. Scott twisted his head and squinted at his surroundings. He was in the shower room. A leaky showerhead *bwopped* water droplets. Someone had finally heard him. A coach, a custodian.

"Hey! Help! I'm in here!"

Bwop.

"I know where you are, Scott."

Bwop.

Someone entered the shower room and passed through his field of vision too fast to identify, and laid something down on the floor before him. The electric air pump Coach used to prime the soccer balls.

Bwop.

"Can you help me? Someone left me here wrapped in this net."

The person crouched down and whispered in his ear.

"That would be me."

The voice. He knew that voice.

Bwop.

"People say you have a big head, Scott. But it could get bigger."

The air pump's needle was rammed into his neck. It was not designed to break skin, and bent slightly, threatening to snap, before stiffening and sinking deep into his flesh. It took a moment for the sensation of pressure to become one of pain. Scott wanted to scream but could do little more than gurgle. Something was filling his throat, fast.

Blood.

The pump was triggered, and air bubbles the size of coffee crystals flooded his carotid artery and zoomed up, brain-bound.

"Please!" he choked. "Stop! I'll do anything! I'll asdfgds —" Bubbles lodged in his cerebrum, short-circuiting his power of speech. His body went limp.

Bwop.

A troop of smaller, deadly bubbles hunkered down in his brain. Everything started to go dark in Scott's eyes as his heart stopped and his lungs begged for air that wasn't coming. In the corner of the shower room was a soccer ball. His eyes settled on it.

He died looking at it, wondering who would start center forward now.

Bwop.

Scott Dare

From *Wikipedia*, the free encyclopedia

Scott Dare is an **American** high school student, soccer player, and Grade-A moron. He gained notoriety at **Springfield High School** for setting up his best friend, teammate **Josh Truffle**, in a plagiarism scandal that saw him removed from the team, only to be replaced by Dare himself. Dare self-identified as the school's star **striker**, though the consensus deemed him middling at best.

Fittingly, he died of a swelled head.

CHAPTER 10

The school was closed for the rest of the week while the police investigated the scene.

Cole spent that time in a fog. No baking. No studying. No scheming. Just Cole's thoughts of his classmate, now a corpse, and the people he'd left behind. His parents, who would receive his mail for months, maybe years to come. His friends, who'd hold out on upgrading their phones because they didn't want to lose his goofy jokes, banked in voice-mail messages.

He and Gavin had joked about Scott's death. And then he died. The police were releasing few facts, but Cole couldn't help feeling that he'd somehow set it in motion. "How?" Gavin had asked. "What are you, God? If so, I have a bone to pick with you. If not, don't be stupid. We don't even know what happened."

When the student body was finally allowed to return, the showers in the boys' locker room were still cordoned off with police tape. Complaints of post-gym BO reached a record high and the rule prohibiting body-spray canisters from school grounds was temporarily lifted.

Cole (Lightning in a Bottle) and Gavin (Cool Tsunami) dressed after a dodgeball game, notable for the listlessness of its participants. No one was in much of a mood for violence. All anyone could think about was Scott.

"Dude bit it right over there," said Gavin, nodding at the

bank of showerheads. Cole didn't look. "I heard he was hooked on 'roids, took one injection too many — and burst."

Was he scalded to death by the notoriously temperamental showers?

Had he slipped, his cantaloupe head rupturing merrily on impact?

Or was his death the consequence of some arcane hazing rite gone awry?

Details were still few. The police refused to comment before results of the autopsy were in. With nothing to go on, Springfield speculated. "One thing's for sure," said Gavin. "He left quite the mess. Can you imagine taking a shower in there now?"

Scott was in the shower, Scott was in gym class, Scott was everywhere. At his locker, in the makeshift memorial of candles, teddy bears, and yearbook photos. In the hallways and the cafeteria and the library, in the cracked faces of the girls who hadn't known they'd crushed on him until he wasn't around to be crushed upon. On the black armbands worn by the soccer team, whose season was now officially in jeopardy. In the words of the teachers, all of whom had taken a crash course in grief counseling the day before.

One of whom was eager to put his newly acquired skills for empathy to good use. Chetley had abandoned his lesson exploring HTML in favor of exploring the grieving process. "We've experienced a tragedy," he began class. On the chalkboard he'd written the word *catharsis*. He was wearing an armband, too. "And we need to talk it out."

"Watch us grieve our way to Thanksgiving break without a class," murmured Gavin.

"I was on Twitter when the news hit," said Chetley. "I couldn't believe it. It was a bad joke. But a look at my Twitter timeline confirmed it. Every post for miles around was hash-tagged DareIsDead. I went numb." Chetley placed his hands on the back of Scott's empty chair. "I say we change that. I say from now on we hashtag DareToDream."

"You could tell by looking at that there was a lot going on," said one student, eager to get in on the emoting. "Scott was a sensitive guy. He was real. And complicated."

This offended Gavin most of all. "Come on. Let's be real. Scott was about as complicated as algae."

Chetley looked up from doling comfort. "That's enough, Gavver."

But it wasn't enough for Gavin. "Just because Scott is dead doesn't mean he's worthy of our tears. He was an overprivi-leged, under-talented aspiring bully and professional cheat. The only person I can think of at this school qualified to refute that is Josh Truffle. If I find out that he's grieving the loss of the guy who stole his spot on the soccer team and may have cost him his shot at college, so will I."

Cole wondered the same thing, and so was someone else. Lila tracked him down in the cafeteria, where the lunch staff ladled out gloppy helpings of spaghetti.

"I figured a foodie like you would brown-bag it," she said, accompanying him to the table he shared with Gavin.

"I always suspected the sudden death of a peer would throw me off my game. Now I know it's true." Why did Cole feel the need to be quippy around her?

"For you and others, it would seem." She didn't ask to join them, but Gavin was in no position to deny her a seat with a forkful of noodles in his mouth. Also, she was a girl, and welcome by nature. "My sources say Winnie was so distraught she had to beg her English teacher for an extension on a paper due today. That's not like her, is it?"

Of course it wasn't. "Why do you care? Are you writing an article about her?"

Lila glanced at Gavin.

"It's cool," said Cole. "You can trust him. Gavin, Lila. Aka Walda Winchell."

"Charmed," said Gavin, offering his hand. Lila regarded it as though it were sticky with syrup, but took it anyway and squeezed — hard. "Big fan," he squeaked as she pulverized his hand.

"You were saying? About this article?"

"I'm writing *an* article. It's about Scott's death. And the key figures involved."

"Winnie wasn't Scott's friend."

"But Scott was Josh's best friend. And Winnie is Josh's girlfriend."

Cole didn't answer. His attention was on a commotion two tables over.

A trio of soccer players stood next to a woman with a length of shimmery, undulant hair. A cameraman framed the shot as she readied her microphone. "Before we're kicked out would be great." The cameraman nodded.

Lila was fizzing. "What is *she* doing here?"

Local TV news reporter Spring Showers spoke to the camera. "I'm here at Springfield High School, the scene of the gruesome death of senior soccer player Scott Dare."

"Looks like she's getting the story," Gavin said.

"With me are three of his teammates, Harper Caldwell, Wesley O'Shea, and Vincent Cicala. Boys, on behalf of everyone at WSPG, please accept my condolences. We're very sorry for your loss. Can you describe the mood here at SHS?"

"It's pretty . . . bad?"

"Like . . . not good?"

"Everybody's . . . down?"

"I'm sure it has been very hard. How are you coping?"

"It's tough."

"I mean, Scott died."

"Right here in school."

"Do you feel that the administration is doing everything it can to keep you safe?"

It was then that Cole noticed the silence in the cafeteria. There was no eating or chatting. There was only watching.

"Safe from what?" called Gavin.

"Well . . . safe from whoever caused Scott's death." Somewhere in the recesses of the cafeteria, someone dropped a fork. A girl waited for the clattering to stop before making sure everyone heard her whimper. "The coroner is set to release his report today, but I obtained a copy in advance. Right here it says, 'Though his body was severely malformed, it is our opinion that the subject's death was most likely the result of another party's action.' Apparently someone used an air pump to . . . pump him up."

Dead silence.

Then the bell screeched, and so did everyone in the cafeteria.

The cameraman panned across the tables, capturing the usual post-bell hullaballoo hullaballooning out of control, the students near riot, surging with the fear that a killer was among them. Cole's body was motionless but his mind was galloping as everyone streamed out the doors, into the hallways, and out the exits, overwhelming hall monitors. The principal fought his way inside against the flow and stomped toward Spring. In her haste to flee, she dropped the coroner's report. Cole pocketed it and ducked into an alcove. He was well into a second read when Gavin found him. "It's chaos! Let's ditch before the faculty regains control!" Cole didn't move, stuck on a passage in the report. "What is the matter with you?"

Cole stooped against an overturned table. "Scott stroked out. That's what killed him."

"I thought it was an air pump."

"The air pump shot air into his brain. The air caused the stroke. The stroke did him in."

"You're making me feel dumb. If you have a point, spit it out."

"Air bubbles in the brain. Does that mean anything to you?"

"Should it?"

"Yeah. 'Cause we wrote it."

CHAPTER 11

*T*hat is the stupidest thing I have ever heard," Gavin said. He and Cole had retreated to their lockers after the mayhem in the cafeteria. "Stupider than the fact that *stupidest* is a real word. Scott Dare dies and we predicted it? That's egotistical, even for me. Get over yourself."

Gavin accused Cole of being all these things and more in his epic, steamroller shaming. "We made a joke about someone keeling over, and then that someone keeled over in a vaguely similar manner. That's not murder; that's irony. Or something like it."

"Don't you think it's weird that Scott got turned into a blow-up doll right after we dreamed it up and posted it on the Internet?" Cole asked.

Gavin was willing to acknowledge that much. "But it's not quite as weird as the fact that you think someone went to the trouble of hitching an air pump to his carotid artery when all they had to do to kill him was say 'soccer is for wimps' and watch his head explode. Why copy us? Why kill Scott at all? Who would do that?"

Cole couldn't say Josh's name aloud lest he be branded psycho *and* jealous, so he allowed Gavin the last word.

"Sorry to burst your bubble — pun intended — but the coroner's report wasn't conclusive. It's just as likely Scott died of a freak accident. And even if some nutjob did go after him, the idea that our Wikipedia page was the inspiration is a stretch of G-string proportions. It was a fluke."

Gavin went ahead and skipped. Cole did not have that luxury (it was bouillabaisse day in home ec), so he set himself to auto-student and withdrew inside his head for the rest of the day.

The questions were still niggling when the last bell rang. He drifted along with the students rushing for the buses and was nearly aboard when he saw something in the parking lot that had been missing in the morning. There, among the jalopies and Acuras, was a BMW. Cole turned around and went back inside.

Midway down a corridor across from Chetley's classroom he found Josh's locker. Rummaging through it was Josh.

His usually square and soldierly shoulders were aslant, and his eyes were dull, unlike his hair, which was shiny with grease. He looked less like Josh than Josh's uglier, grieving twin. Or his uglier, guilty twin? Or both?

Cole tested the water. "Hey."

Josh slotted another book into his bag.

"You're here."

"Just to get my assignments." Josh's voice had all the character of an idling engine. There was none of the hostility with which he usually addressed Cole. But then, there was nothing in it to suggest they knew each other at all.

Cole leaned against the lockers, a bro sign for *it's all good.* "All we did in history was more oral reports. Are you coming in tomorrow?"

Josh shook his head. "Scott's memorial."

Cole had never been to a memorial. Or a service. Or a funeral. He pictured a line of students and SHS dignitaries paying respect to Scott's parents, and the casket, dressed in flowers. Would it be closed, the state of Scott's body left to the imagination? Or did the mortician have the power to remold his wattled skin to the bones in his face? What would Cole do if he saw Scott's body? Would he faint? Weep? Shrug?

"I'm supposed to get a picture of Scott and me," Josh said. "For this collage they're going to have at the church. Do you think this is a good one?" He held up a photo that under other, less fatal circumstances would have been destined for the yearbook. Two soccer stars, just guys, mid-celebration after another win.

"Good choice."

Josh pocketed the photo. "Was there something you wanted?"

To look him in the eye? To find out what he's capable of? To learn if Cole was right to be suspicious?

"I wanted to tell you . . . I'm sorry. About Scott."

Josh closed his locker. "I thought you didn't like him."

"I didn't." But he didn't want Scott dead, either. A public pantsing would have sufficed. "But you did. And plenty of other people. I'm sorry for what you're going through." Josh regarded Cole with reserve.

"Thanks." He shouldered his bag but took no step to leave. "I appreciate it." And from the doughy softness in his expression, it seemed like he did. Suddenly Josh looked much more like his former friend than his current adversary, and not at all like a killer.

Through the double doors at the end of the corridor came Winnie, Andrea at her side. Their arms were linked and they slanted against each other in a three-legged shamble. Eyes red with recent tears, they slowed when they saw Cole. It seemed as though a hug was in order, though who should give it and who should receive it was anyone's guess.

"Did you see the counselor?" asked Josh.

Winnie nodded.

"Are you okay?" asked Josh. And Cole. Simultaneously.

She nodded again, gaze flitting from her boyfriend to her ex and back again.

"What is *he* doing here?" asked Andrea.

"I'm talking to Josh." The double doors down the hall behind them opened again. Lila pushed through and halted outside a classroom, a pencil and notepad in her hand as she feigned great interest in a mural. Suddenly Cole could see another *Muckraker* article taking shape, with himself, Winnie, and Josh at the center. "He's all yours," said Cole, pivoting to usher Lila away before she was noticed.

But Andrea wasn't through with him. "Leaving so soon? Without taking another shot at Winnie, even?"

Any thaw between Cole and Josh was flash-frozen. "What is she talking about?" Josh asked Winnie.

Andrea cupped her mouth. "Winnie, you didn't tell him?"

"Don't worry about it, Josh."

Josh did worry about it. "What does 'another shot' mean?"

"I'm so sorry, I thought he knew!" Andrea said.

"Andrea, just stop already!"

"Someone speak!" bellowed Josh.

Cole did. "Great talking to you guys, as always." Josh grabbed Cole by the arm and jerked him back against a locker. Lila's notepad smoked.

"Cole came looking for Winnie the other night at practice," blurted Andrea. "The day you got taken off the team." Josh's fists balled, unballed, and balled again, as he drew his own conclusions.

"Why didn't you tell me?"

"Because it was nothing," Winnie said. "Right, Cole?"

One word from Cole would defuse the situation. Another would light it up. *It was nothing,* Winnie had said.

"I dunno, Winnie," Cole said, his lips moving before his brain had time to exercise veto power. "Sure didn't seem like nothing to me."

Cole cowered, bracing himself for the mashing of bone, but the blow never came. Josh reared back and gave the lockers a free kick instead. From inside came the sound of heavy books pitching over from the tremor. Josh kept kicking, Cole kept cringing, and the lockers kept crashing. Winnie seemed to grow in stature as she shoved herself between Josh and Cole, angrily professing her innocence.

"If nothing really happened, why didn't you just tell me?!" Josh bellowed.

"Maybe because I was trying to keep you from doing something else to justify everyone who is already calling you out!"

Andrea tried to back her up in her own self-serving way. "Don't listen to Cole, he's just trying to cause trouble. I was there when he showed up. I made sure nothing happened."

Josh turned on her. "But you made sure I found out, didn't you? You don't care what goes on between Winnie and me, you just care that something goes on. Anything that creates a little drama and draws attention from your miserable little dead-end existence. I'm done being your entertainment."

Josh didn't stick around to subject himself to Andrea's indignation. Neither did Winnie. "I'll talk to you later," she said, tramping off in the other direction. Of the three of them left, none quite believed it.

Cole released a chuckle, amazed he was alive, and even more amazed that he had not soiled himself. Andrea swept to his face. No girl had been closer to him since the last time Winnie had kissed him. "You won't think you're so funny when I'm through with you." Then she was gone.

Lila was still jotting when Cole swiped her notebook and tore out the related pages. "I gave you one story. You give me one." He walked away.

"I'm not your enemy, Cole," she called. "But Andrea is."

CHAPTER 12

Andrea got no joy from collecting the mail at home every day. Once a month she'd receive a magazine and her medication but the important stuff came delivered directly to her iPad: birthday money, rumors, and the latest embarrassing selfie making the rounds.

Still, bringing in the mail was the only contribution to the household her mother asked her to make, so she did it without complaint.

Andrea knew she had it pretty good, even if her *pretty good* had come at a cost. Since their divorce, her parents had gone out of their way to lower their expectations of her behavior. And since her father's death those expectations had crashed right through the floor.

He'd been a fixture on the local news since before she was born. "Cal, the Winking Weatherman," they'd called him. Then one day, not long ago, he'd been killed in a freak accident by one of his own props. The wiring holding a lightning bolt to the rigging above the set broke loose. The lightning bolt plunged directly into his wink-eye. "He never saw it coming," Andrea overheard the anchor tell Spring Showers at the wake. His death had been ruled an accident, but that hadn't stopped Spring from asking Andrea if he'd had enemies.

"Just the scale," Andrea had replied.

He was gone but condolences from disturbed viewers

continued to pour in. She sifted through them and had helped herself to every credit card offered to her mother. Now her wallet was packed with two Visas, two MasterCards, one AmEx, and a Discover. But who took Discover?

Andrea learned other things from getting first crack at the mail. Things her mother wouldn't share with her, things involving the phrases *past due*, *third notice*, and *collection agency*.

Besides the refill of her medication, today's haul included a letter from the lawyer handling her father's estate. Andrea steamed it open and read that her father's other ex-wives were contesting the will. She restuffed the envelope and stuck it at the bottom of the pile, wondering, *Maybe the electric company takes Discover.*

Alone in the house.

She could do homework, but why bother?

She could watch TV, but TV was terrible.

She could have something to eat, but that would be eating.

She checked her e-mail. Nothing from Winnie. Nothing on Twitter or Facebook. Nothing from anyone. She'd checked it all on her phone two minutes ago.

Two minutes is long enough to wait before refreshing.

Your miserable little dead-end existence . . .

Her mother wouldn't be home from work for hours. She set Pandora to Robyn and turned up the volume before scrolling through the contacts in her phone. She could try Winnie again. She'd tried once before and was ignored. Try again and she'd look desperate. What if Winnie was with some other friend when the call came through? What if she wondered aloud why some people could not get the hint? Andrea put her phone down.

Your miserable little dead-end existence . . .

She hated Josh. She hadn't always. But she hated him now. She hated Cole, too. Equally smitten with Winnie, slobbery Cole was at least controllable. He was socially stunted and only moderately attractive in that dull, Labrador retriever kind of way. And because he never dreamed he could do better, he sponged up abuse with a laugh, as if in on a joke no one even told, counting himself lucky to be in the presence of girls at all. Cole reminded her of her father, near the end, although by the time of his death he'd gotten a backbone and tried to clamp down on her social life, as if he could do that. Still, he was dead, and that wasn't the greatest.

She felt a hitch in the back of her throat, and her face scrunched up in advance of coming tears.

Nothing came.

Your miserable little dead-end existence . . .

Winnie wasn't the only one who could evolve. Andrea could reinvent herself, too.

She cruised Reddit for a while, sorting through responses to her IAmA personas.

IAmA shark attack survivor.

IAmA exorcist.

IAmA human sushi platter.

Each identity was carefully researched, fully realized, and honed to the finest detail. Her online readers believed everything she wrote. And they wanted to know more.

IAmA daughter NOT in mourning. My father died. I don't miss him.

Her true story had the most upvotes. People were concerned about her state of mind. Some of them thought she was depressed, others thought she was dangerous. A father's death should count for something, they said.

Your miserable little dead-end existence . . .

With an audience, it was easier. She played a role, an imaginary version of herself, like one of her IAmA creations. *IAmA daughter who misses her father* cried on cue. To do anything other than weep would be out of character, or strange. No one in high school could afford that label. So she mustered tears where necessary. But generating them when alone was another matter. She knew what others expected of her but did not know what she expected of herself. In the privacy of her room she wondered if it mattered to her that her father was dead or if she simply did not have any tears left.

Her mother called this nonsense but begged a prescription from a doctor friend anyway. The medicine was sent in an eye-dropper and was marketed to sufferers of something called Chronic Dry Eye. Andrea looked at her phone again to make sure it wasn't set to vibrate. Had she missed a call?

No. The ringer was on full blast. Now she definitely felt like crying.

Your miserable little dead-end existence . . .

She would call Winnie again. Who cares if she came off as pitiful? They would talk it out. Andrea would confide everything in her. They'd have a good cry and everything would be okay. She retrieved her prescription refill and went into the bathroom to get ready.

The package was lined with USPS tape. *We're sorry. Your package was damaged in shipment.* Andrea tore it open and removed the dropper. One drop per eye was adequate.

She shouldn't have opened her mouth like that in front of Josh.

She uncapped the dropper.

Next time she'll think before she speaks.

She tilted her head back and raised the dropper.

She and Winnie were best friends. For now, at least. They didn't let stupid Cole come between them. And they wouldn't let Josh do it, either.

She gently pried apart her eyelids, exposing the ball.

Winnie would make Josh apologize to Andrea. And be nice to her.

She positioned the dropper over her eye and squeezed. A glob formed at the end of the spout.

Or she would not be nice to Josh.

The medicine kerplunked onto her eye and frothed on contact.

Her eye sizzled.

A wisp of vapor, like dry ice, curled off its surface.

Her eye began to melt, and Andrea screamed.

Your miserable little dead-end existence . . .

Winnie Hoffman @WinWin100

@hendersdaughter Andrea we love you

10 minutes ago Favorite Retweet Reply

Andrea Henderson @hendersdaughter

Please keep her in your thoughts and prayers

12 minutes ago Favorite Retweet Reply

Andrea Henderson @hendersdaughter

And the next couple of days will be very important

13 minutes ago Favorite Retweet Reply

Andrea Henderson @hendersdaughter

She is in serious condition

13 minutes ago Favorite Retweet Reply

Andrea Henderson @hendersdaughter

They had to take it out

15 minutes ago Favorite Retweet Reply

Andrea Henderson @hendersdaughter

She had to have emergency surgery on her eye
last night

15 minutes ago Favorite Retweet Reply

Andrea Henderson @hendersdaughter

I know many of you are concerned about Andrea

16 minutes ago Favorite Retweet Reply

Andrea Henderson @hendersdaughter

This is Andrea's mom

16 minutes ago   Favorite Retweet Reply

Winnie Hoffman @WinWin100

@hendersdaughter I texted you. Where r u?

18 hours ago   Favorite Retweet Reply

Andrea Henderson @hendersdaughter

@ABrindleDocent Blocked

20 hours ago   Favorite Retweet Reply

Rabid Doc Lenten @ABrindleDocent

@hendersdaughter we will see about that

21 hours ago   Favorite Retweet Reply

Andrea Henderson @hendersdaughter

@ABrindleDocent I don't cry that much lol

21 hours ago   Favorite Retweet Reply

Andrea Henderson @hendersdaughter

@ABrindleDocent Do I know you?

20 hours ago   Favorite Retweet Reply

Rabid Doc Lenten @ABrindleDocent

@hendersdaughter you cry a lot

21 hours ago   Favorite Retweet Reply

Andrea Henderson

From *Wikipedia*, the free encyclopedia

Andrea Henderson is an **American** high school student best known for being the daughter of **Cal Henderson**, a fat, crazy, crazy-fat weatherman who died live on camera. Andrea is also noted for her inability to go a single day without crying over something.

She died crying her eyes out.

CHAPTER 13

Gavin and Cole sat astride their bicycles. A chalky sky idled over Andrea's house.

"This is a mistake," gloomed Gavin. "Being here is the act of a guilty person."

Cole dismounted. "Then I'm in the right place." He took a package out of his backpack, looked up at the house, and hesitated.

"I don't have a note."

"So?"

"I can't leave this without a note, can I?"

"Yeah, you don't want to be impolite to the half-blind girl," Gavin replied. "Let's draft something. 'Dear Cyclops, I mean, Andrea. Sorry about your eye. But did you know? The pirate look is back! For a preppy twist, try an eye patch with a tartan print.' Can we go now?"

Cole crept to the porch, noteless. The lights were off inside. He stared up at the door. The door stared back. Was it inviting him to come closer, or daring him?

Gavin pee-danced on the sidewalk. "What are you waiting for? Do it before someone sees."

Cole climbed the steps and saw he wasn't the first to arrive. The porch was piled high with casseroles, wedges of lasagna, and pulpy potato salads. No pastries, though. Cole gave his tin of compost cookies a place of prominence, balancing it on top of the food tower, which promptly tipped over. A light clicked on inside the house.

"Book it!" cried Gavin, already pedaling.

Cole had one leg cast over his bike when he heard the front door bang open. Wheeling off around the corner, he risked a backward glance in time to see a man in a suit emerge and scan the street. Bending over to rearrange the food, his blazer shifted. Something gold glinted from his belt.

"I bet it was a shield," he said to his Coke, blocks later at Benito's. Between Cole and Gavin lay the day's special — a smelt *guanciale* and fennel pie — barely nibbled. Benito watched anxiously from the register for their appetites to make an appearance. "I think that guy was a cop."

Gavin minced a paper napkin. "What would a cop be doing at Andrea's house?"

"Looking for evidence?"

"Evidence of what? Of Andrea's stupidity? Of her breathtakingly vulgar need for attention? Of her illicit stash of spray tanner?"

"Of the person who spiked her eye medicine with sulfuric acid," said Cole.

Gavin released his confettied napkin and sat back. "Would this be the same copycat who turned Scott into an air mattress? Or a different one?"

"We marked people for death! We put it on the Internet for everyone to see! We said Andrea would die crying her eyes out, then she goes and *coincidentally* loses an eye?! How many people have to die by our predictions for you to take it seriously?"

"Only one person is dead," Gavin bit. "Andrea is alive."

Barely. Cole had watched on TV as Spring Showers delivered that scoop from outside the hospital.

"The victim was treated at Springfield General, where she clings to life. Loved ones have been trickling into the hospital all day."

Dropped among the shots of assorted Hendersons plodding bravely into the hospital was a snippet of a familiar concave be-cardiganed chest. Cole wasn't sure what surprised him more: that Chetley knew Andrea well enough to visit her bedside or that he didn't stop to opine on her calamity for the camera. Then Winnie appeared, darting through the shot.

Josh was nowhere to be seen as Spring shadowed her to the door, dangling a microphone for comment. Winnie kept her head down and her mouth shut as she hurried by. Cole found himself pausing the playback. Grief and a plasma screen seemed to bring her beauty into even sharper focus.

"In addition to losing her eye, Henderson is said to have sustained third-degree chemical burns over thirty percent of her face. Authorities are stymied as to whether her eye medication was contaminated — or laced — with acid. The accident marks the second tragedy to befall the Springfield High School community following the recent gruesome death of Scott Dare."

Losing her eye.

Chemical burns.

Second tragedy.

"Andrea was lucky her mom found her before her face melted clean off. But if that hadn't happened, she'd have died," Cole said, "just the way we said she would." Gavin stood up. "Where are you going?"

84

"Home. Gonna whip up my own profile. If I'm not in school tomorrow, it's because I'm de-virginizing myself on a bed of a hundred million dollars I won in the lottery. You know, because of our magical ability to Wiki things into happening." Gavin left Cole with the uneaten pizza and unanswered questions.

Was he even a little bit to blame for Scott's death and Andrea's disfigurement? Or were their grisly fates just a *Final Destination* rip-off? Why did the knot in his gut tell him it was something worse? Could it get any worse than those movies?

Cole did not want to find out. He went home, where distractions were plenty. He had work to do. Work to win valedictorian, work to achieve the bright future his parents envisioned for him, a future that would shape up to a perfectly respectable Wikipedia profile of his own. An array of assignments loomed, neglected since Scott's death. Stacked neatly on his desk were his college essays, freshly edited by the wannabe professor hired by his parents. They would expect revised drafts in a day's time. A new issue of *Cook's Illustrated* flirted from his nightstand. There was plenty to occupy his thoughts. He popped a Red Bull and awoke his laptop. Open on his screen were Wikipedia and Twitter. His timeline was all Andrea.

Andrea Henderson @hendersdaughter
@Springfield And for your cookies.
44 minutes ago Favorite Retweet Reply

Andrea Henderson @hendersdaughter
@Springfield Thank you for all your support.
45 minutes Favorite Retweet Reply

Andrea Henderson @hendersdaughter

@Springfield But we're in good spirits.

56 minutes ago   Favorite Retweet Reply

Andrea Henderson @hendersdaughter

@Springfield Not to mention a prosthetic eye.

57 minutes ago   Favorite Retweet Reply

Andrea Henderson @hendersdaughter

@Springfield Next up is facial reconstruction.

57 minutes ago   Favorite Retweet Reply

Andrea Henderson @hendersdaughter

@Springfield There is still a ways to go.

58 minutes ago   Favorite Retweet Reply

Andrea Henderson @hendersdaughter

@Springfield In fact she's already itching to get on Facebook!

59 minutes ago   Favorite Retweet Reply

Andrea Henderson @hendersdaughter

@Springfield Andrea is awake and doing well.

59 minutes ago   Favorite Retweet Reply

Andrea Henderson @hendersdaughter

@Springfield I have good news.

1 hour ago Favorite Retweet Reply

Rabid Doc Lenten @ABrindleDocent

@hendersdaughter pulling for andrea

2 hours ago   Favorite Retweet Reply

Winnie Hoffman @WinWin100

@hendersdaughter If we can help in any way
please just say so

8 hours ago   Favorite Retweet Reply

So.

Andrea would be okay.

Except for the horrible burns and disfiguring scars and glass eye and psychic pain.

But still!

So why didn't Cole feel much better?

His knee was bouncing. The Red Bull had begun to work its syrupy voodoo. A thought thwapped around in his head, a bat trapped in an attic. The Tweets in support of Andrea numbered in the thousands, but something about Rabid Doc Lenten/ABrindleDocent stood out. Cole called up an anagram server and entered the Twitter handle. The results topped sixty-five thousand, but he was only looking for one, one in particular, and he found it before scrolling through the first thousand: *Rabid Doc Lenten*. Neither phrase meant much of anything, and he didn't know anyone by the last name *Lenten*. There was something about it, something familiar, something he couldn't put a finger on.

He put his fingers to use elsewhere, on the keyboard, and let fly. Soon he had laid out whole bricks of text.

His assignments remained untouched; Wikipedia did not. Cole stayed up through the night, deleting, researching, rewriting all the profiles he and Gavin had unleashed. As night gave way to morning, each offensive passage and demise was stripped and replaced with just-the-facts-ma'am truth about his targets. It was only a small, cookie-sized token of remorse, but it felt good. Like he'd done something, however negligible, to right a wrong . . . and take himself off the hook for the violence he feared he was responsible for. He got his first wink of sleep on the bus. Everything would be okay.

Cole was an ace of a lot of things. Fooling himself was one of them.

CHAPTER 14

Cole lost himself in the stacks of the SHS library before class and tried to catch up on sleep. Someone else had other plans for his day.

A pleasing aroma brought him around. It did not belong amidst the scents of remnant carpet and neglected volumes. Chocolate chip. Oatmeal. Brown sugar, butter, Raisinets, and pretzels, all mixed together — no, not pretzels. Stupid Cole. Something saltier. A potato chip.

He knew this scent.

Cole opened his eyes. Sitting on the floor next to him was Lila, wearing a faux-Victorian dress with black lace-up boots, thick-soled and suctioned to her calves like leeches. Her fingers and wrists and earlobes and neck were riddled with a collection of metallic accessories, all buckles and gears, as though she'd thrown herself on a Steampunk nail bomb. On another girl the display might be a costume, or armor, or bait. But Lila wore it casually, like a bathrobe. A fresh notepad was nearby, but in her hand she held the two remaining bites of a cookie.

"Potato chip in a cookie," she munched. "Who knew?"

"What period is it?" he asked.

Lila took a bite of cookie and shrugged. "I considered waking you up. But it looked like you needed the rest. Long night?"

"Who wants to know? Lila? Or Walda?"

"As if either one of us would waste our time on a story about sleep-deprived students."

"Then why watch me sleep?" He regretted the question as soon as he asked it.

Lila tongued a gunk of cookie from the reaches of her mouth and swallowed. "Why do people watch the ocean? Or a monkey with a gun?" she said, leading with her chin. "Sooner or later you know it's going to do something interesting."

Cole felt the stack looming behind him, high, like his rising temperature. Lila seemed to have a knack for showing up at vulnerable moments, almost as if she was watching him. He wondered how much she knew about the Wikipedia pages.

"Besides," said Lila, "I saw you here and thought you were waiting for me. After all, it is our place." Cole caught sight of a collection of Goethe and only just realized which deserted section he'd plopped down in. *"Richtig,"* said Lila, her voice lilting. *"Poesie."*

"I — I was tired," he stammered. "I wanted some quiet."

Lila did nothing to hide her disappointment. "Then you could use an energy boost. Cookie?" she offered.

The cookie.

"I know what it tastes like. I conceived of the recipe. I bought the ingredients. I mixed them together. I baked it. For myself."

"Funny," said Lila, "when I saw you leave them on Andrea's porch yesterday I just assumed you baked them for her mom." That answered the question of whether or not she was watching him. "Of course, I had to wait for the police to leave before finding out exactly what you'd put there. Do you have any idea how hard it was to wait that long? Harder than waiting for the next installment of *Game of Thrones*. But it was that or get caught staking the place out. Like you and Gavin did."

"You were there?!" Of lesser importance: Lila was into *Game of Thrones*?!

She didn't even bother to nod. "I spent my time hiding in the bushes pondering another question."

"What is the sentence for cookie-theft?"

"I only took a few. Wish I'd taken the whole batch. Pastries are wasted on the grieving." Lila read from her notepad. " 'What did Gavin mean when he told Cole that being at Andrea's house was the act of a guilty man? And what did Cole mean when he said: "Then I'm in the right place?" ' "

This was the moment in those crime procedurals in which the suspect requests a lawyer.

"At first I wrote it off as garden-variety remorse. Whether you like her or not, everybody feels bad about what happened to Andrea, and there's nothing sinister about homemade cookies."

Could she know?

"But something was nagging, and it wasn't until I woke up this morning that I knew what that something was."

She couldn't know.

"It was the tip you gave me about Scott Dare's Wikipedia page. There was something in it I hadn't mentioned in my article."

Please don't let her know.

"The profile predicted the manner of Scott's death."

She knew. Maybe not everything, but plenty. Enough to put her on his trail. Cole's insides electrified. He needed to get away. He needed to put as much distance between him and Lila as possible.

But another part, a part that was growing louder and more insistent every day, needed to confess. That part of him needed to be unburdened, no matter what the consequences. That part of him needed to stop lying. He didn't know which part would win out.

"That made me curious," said Lila. "So when I got here this morning I went online and found Andrea's profile." She leaned in, confidential. "Nasty piece of work. Whoever is chronicling her life sure has an ax to grind. But I was wondering if losing her eye was predicted as well. Sure enough, it was in there. Except there was no way of knowing whether it existed before or after the incident. According to the history of changes, the Wikipedia profile was last edited as recently as first period."

Cole blinked. "First period yesterday, you mean?"

"No. First period today. This morning."

Cole hadn't touched the profile since last night.

He dashed down the aisle and made for the exit.

"Where are you going?" called Andrea.

Cole bypassed the library's computers and shot top-speed for the computer lab, hoping Lila wouldn't be caught dead running, like every other girl he knew (though, to be fair, he didn't know many). By the time he arrived there was no sign of her, nor anyone else. Cole knew Chetley's classroom would be empty. He had lunch-monitor duty, floating from table to table in search of an invitation to sit down. Cole would have the space to himself until next period.

It was dark inside, except for the dim glow of a single monitor, its screensaver emitting the only light. Cole swiped at the mouse, ready to call up Wikipedia —

But it was already done for him. Someone else had been reading SHS Wikipedia profiles and left them open on the desktop.

Scott's profile, Andrea's profile, and the rest.

And just like Lila said, each had been restored to its original, pre-sanitized version. Every glib remark, every vicious story, every sick rumor.

Every gruesome death.

CHAPTER 15

Winnie had once coaxed Cole into joining her for a yoga class, but he hadn't gone back a second time. He couldn't maintain focus during the poky exercise, and he didn't like the moistness of the mats or the way he looked in caterpillar pose. Serenity hadn't been for him. But sitting there in Chetley's classroom, staring at the monitor full of his make-believe slaughter come back to haunt him, he felt different.

He tried to remember the yoga breathing and regain his composure.

Be calm.

Don't panic.

You are trained in the Socratic method.

You are no stranger to deductive reasoning.

You are the valedictorian.

Well, you will be.

(Hopefully)

You can figure this out.

Cole sat back from the computer, a thousand questions jigging in his head.

Jiggiest among them:

What on earth is going on?

Someone had killed Scott and tried to kill Andrea. That someone was following the innocent revenge scenarios he'd laid out on their Wikipedia profiles. That someone wasn't going to let him forget it, and wasn't going to let his work disappear from the Internet. And that someone might not be satisfied with just Scott and Andrea. That someone might go after the others. Drick. Josh.

Winnie.

So who was it?

Cole knew the answer was right in front of him. In Wikipedia. He clenched his abs, settled himself, and took a closer look at the top profile: Andrea's. The cursor blinked in an open field.

It hit Cole.

The last user wasn't just reading the profiles.

The last user was logged into them.

Editing them.

Adding to them.

Was the last user their killer?

Cole didn't have time to find out. Whoever had been here was gone now, but wouldn't have left the pages open and logged into. Whoever it was expected to be back — and soon.

Cole acted fast.

Check the edit history. Find the username.

The computer's clock wormed closer to the end of the period. Cole scrolled to the top of the page and scanned the heading for the culprit's username.

Then he found it. And there would be no mistaking it.

The doorknob jostled.

Cole dove for cover behind Chetley's desk and clonked the side of his head in the process. Pain tore down his scalp as he crammed himself into a ball. Why was he hiding? It was the middle of the day in the middle of school. What could happen to him here?

Maybe Scott had wondered the same thing before someone gifted him with a new orifice.

The door swung open.

The lights stayed off.

Footsteps.

From his vantage Cole watched as a pair of legs strode through the room and came to a sudden stop just outside kicking distance of his face. He held his backpack closer, held his breath, held on for dear life as the interloper paused.

The computer Cole had abandoned glowed brightly, the Wikipedia profiles gesturing rudely. He hadn't toggled the screen saver back into use, hadn't even thought to do so. Now it was too late.

The steps resumed, but slower, as even and deliberate as the stroke of a pendulum, on a direct course for the computer and Cole's undoing.

He took a mental inventory of the objects at his disposal and their potential application for self-defense: books, paper, stubby pencils. Unless Cole could inflict death by paper cut, he was in no position to fight for his life.

The only thing to do was run. He could cross the room in four, maybe five leaps, but an obstacle course of desks and chairs lay between him and escape. He would have to be chimp-nimble. Cole arranged himself into a three-point stance, ready to spring.

But if he was caught, what then?

Detention?

Shame?

Only if the person at the computer wasn't a killer.

If it was . . . Cole would be victim number three.

The bell tolled. The period had ended. Class was over.

The visitor's feet pivoted in the direction of the door. Two seconds passed. Fads, genres, dynasties lived and died in the five long seconds before the scattered voices of the first students exiting their classrooms grew into a thrum.

Cole was frozen. The visitor hovered before the computer for another moment. Keystrokes. The click of the mouse. The shut-down sigh of the computer. Exiting footsteps. The door closing.

Cole gophered his head above the tabletop. He was alone with his thoughts, weedy with questions. One of them stuck out. The only one with an answer.

Question: Who had been logged in and editing?

Answer: PainAuChoCOLEat.

Whoever was logged in was logged in as Cole.

Which meant that whoever was logged in was setting him up.

So far, one murder and one maiming had been scored in his name.

How many others would die before it all came to an end?

CHAPTER 16

Cole retreated to a stall in a boys' bathroom notorious for its bomb shelter ventilation. There he could think in relatively undisturbed, if toxic, peace. Cheap jokes at Drick's expense were scrawled across the inside of the stall. Cole was absent from history, a first for him. He'd never skipped any class, ever, and in one day had managed to skip every single one. But a twinge of guilt beat death or mutilation, although having his head messed with was not exactly pleasant, either.

Someone had logged onto Wikipedia using his handle and reconstituted the pages he'd taken down. But who would go to such great lengths to mess with him? What had he ever done to anyone?

Plenty.

He didn't know where to start. But Gavin might. If anyone could summon up and whittle down a field of suspects, it was him. Assuming he could stop himself from laughing at the story long enough to think about it. As the period drew to a close, Cole braved the halls and headed for history.

When Gavin emerged from class, Cole was waiting for him.

"Congratulations on picking the best day ever to skip class," he grumbled. In his hand was the carcass of his term paper on Benedict Arnold, all red ink and exclamation marks. "I know it isn't my best work but why can't Drick take into account we're all suffering from an epidemic of tragedy? I could get mauled by a baboon today, and tomorrow he'd still deduct five points for improper citation."

Cole drew Gavin aside, his nerves swelling.

"And don't assume you're immune. Your homemade crullers will only buy you so much goodwill. There's a special place in community college for top-ten-percenters who slack off before the last semester."

"It's top one-percent, thank you, and right now I'm more concerned with preserving my sanity than my rank."

This got Gavin's attention. Like any good historian, he was always up for a story of downfall. "Last night I revised the Wiki pages. Cleaned them up. Got rid of all the nasty bits. But this morning they were back exactly how I first wrote them. And whoever restored them used my own log-in to do it. I think whoever did it maybe killed Scott and tried to do the same to Andrea, too."

Gavin was, for once, speechless.

That lasted two seconds.

"Wow. Okay. You weren't kidding about the sanity thing." He twirled his bangs, thinking. "This requires brainstorming. And a branzino pizza pie. To Benito's." Cole and Gavin took a step in unison when Winnie appeared, and Cole stopped. He could not remember the last time he'd encountered her without minders. Would she rip into him? Ignore him? Not notice him at all? This was not really the time to explore the latest developments in their romantic saga, but Cole didn't know how to walk away from her, either.

Gavin knew better than to waste time dissuading Cole from interacting with Winnie and said they'd talk later before offering a not-so-friendly reminder. "Don't forget you hate her."

Winnie stepped up to Cole, as though walking a tightrope. Not one moment ago Gavin had said something, something he ought to remember. It eluded him now.

"You missed class."

She'd noticed?

"I'm sure I didn't miss much," he replied. His feet were splayed and his weight concentrated in one hip, allowing the other to jut, lazy and available. He'd lifted the look from Josh and spent many post-shower, towel-clad moments practicing it before a full-length mirror. He never dreamed he could pull it off in public, but he never dreamed he could skip class, either. "Sometimes you just need a break, you know?"

Winnie looked away. "Yeah. I guess I do."

Of course she knew, idiot. Her best friend almost died. School probably felt like a vacation from the burn unit.

"I saw you on TV," Cole divulged. Winnie's eyes wandered back to meet his. "When you went to see Andrea at the hospital. Is she doing any better?"

"Her mother says so. I wish I could make that call myself. I wasn't allowed in to see her. I don't think Andrea wants company."

Cole couldn't blame her. Last night he did a Google image search for *acid burns*. He'd never cook liver again.

"Give her time. She'll need her friend back."

"I hope so. I need her back." Here, Winnie paused. "But maybe she's getting all the support she needs from you."

Huh?

"I sat with her mom for a while. She offered me a cookie from the food people dropped off at their house. I knew it was your baking as soon as I tasted the Rollo. Mrs. Henderson is a fan. She wishes she could write a thank-you card to the baker. Strangely, he didn't leave a note."

Cole shifted uncomfortably. "You could've told her it was me."

"But then she might have asked me why my ex-boyfriend was leaving cookies for her. And I wouldn't know what to say." Neither would Cole. "Except that it was very nice of him."

That might have been a compliment. "Why are we talking?" asked Cole.

"I don't know," said Winnie. "Because people talk?" She stood at an angle to him, half of her positioned to make a break for it, half of her positioned to make a stand. As if she had a decision to make. As if she hadn't already made it.

"Not us," said Cole. "That was your choice. Not mine."

"Then stop talking to me." Check and mate.

A crash inside Drick's room jolted them. The din of the hallway receded, absorbed it, and resumed, unstoppable. Winnie and Cole looked inside.

Drick's desk was on its side. Loose essays blanketed the floor. An upturned box of chalk had opened in the tumult, its contents still rolled between chairs in a race. Drick stood on one side of the desk, his knuckles on his hips, silent but unperturbed by the mess. Josh stood on the other side, his shoulders heaving beneath his tank top.

Isn't he cold? thought Cole.

"I shouldn't have done that, oh my God, I didn't mean to do that." The words blundered from Josh's clown-car mouth. "I'm sorry."

"We'll continue this conversation with the principal. And your parents."

Josh's face flushed. "You can't do this to me."

Drick groaned to one knee, gathering up the disorder. "Run along, Josh."

Josh dropped to help, grabbing fistfuls of papers, creasing them. Cole spotted his own assignment among them. An *85* in red. Cole had never seen an *8* in the tens' place before. A *5*, in any position, was also rare. Before the significance of the abysmal grade could sink in, he noticed something else: The *5* was shades darker than the *8*. It was wet.

Josh was crying over it.

"Mr. Drick, you don't understand. I can't afford this. Academic probation has already knocked me down the depth charts of every college I want to go to. If my grades get worse, I'm off them altogether!"

"You should have considered that before you cheated."

"It was one time! This isn't fair," Josh wailed, his young man's voice incongruous with the tantrum. "Can't you cut me some slack? My best friend just got killed and you're holding my whole future hostage!"

Drick sat back on his haunches and looked at Josh mildly, not uncaring. He put his hand on Josh's shoulder. "I know it's hard to believe this now, but there are many futures. I promise, whichever one finds you, it will be good. Even if it doesn't include soccer."

Josh's eyes went dry. He grabbed Drick by the lapels and cast him down with force, the spindly teacher rag-dolling to the floor. Josh rose to his feet, wiping his face. "If I don't have soccer, there is no future for me. Or for you."

CHAPTER 17

ShesGottaGavlt: i always miss the good stuff

PainAuChoCOLEat: Lila will cover it in the Muckraker tomorrow.

PainAuChoCOLEat: That's almost like being there.

PainAuChoCOLEat: Besides, I'm sure Josh isn't done melting down.

ShesGottaGavlt: especially if drick keeps up his new scoring system

PainAuChoCOLEat: What new scoring system?

PainAuChoCOLEat: He has a new scoring system??

ShesGottaGavlt: yeah

ShesGottaGavlt: fail everybody

ShesGottaGavlt: speaking of

ShesGottaGavlt: what did you get on your paper

PainAuChoCOLEat: I don't want to talk about it.

ShesGottaGavlt: uh oh

ShesGottaGavlt: trouble in ivytown

PainAuChoCOLEat: It's no big deal.

ShesGottaGavlt: hope you applied to some safety schools

PainAuChoCOLEat: It's one grade.

ShesGottaGavlt: you could always join the merchant marines

PainAuChoCOLEat: I will handle Drick.

PainAuChoCOLEat: You handle your assignment.

PainAuChoCOLEat: I need your assessment of my Wikipedia situation.

ShesGottaGavlt: my assessment is you got hacked

PainAuChoCOLEat: How astute of you.

ShesGottaGavlt: hey, i spent my valuable time considering the ins and outs of your persecution complex

ShesGottaGavlt: by mySELF

PainAuChoCOLEat: You spent the afternoon pondering and this is all you came up with? I'm being hacked?

ShesGottaGavlt: please deposit gratitude and proof of friendship for further analysis

PainAuChoCOLEat: Give me something to be grateful for.

PainAuChoCOLEat: Tell me who is messing with me.

ShesGottaGavlt: you are the top one percent

ShesGottaGavlt: you might be the valedictorian

ShesGottaGavlt: you tell me

PainAuChoCOLEat: If I had the slightest idea, I wouldn't be asking you.

ShesGottaGavlt: are you really saying you cannot figure this out

ShesGottaGavlt: its obvious

ShesGottaGavlt: the person who hacked you

ShesGottaGavlt: the person who restored the wikis

ShesGottaGavlt: the person behind it all

ShesGottaGavlt: is

ShesGottaGavlt: WHINNY

PainAuChoCOLEat: WHAT?

ShesGottaGavlt: to wit

ShesGottaGavlt: she wants to make you carayzee

ShesGottaGavlt: keep you distracted while she sneaks up on you

ShesGottaGavlt: uses her GPA to club you over the head all baby seal like

ShesGottaGavlt: and take valedictorian for her diabolical self

PainAuChoCOLEat: Seriously?

PainAuChoCOLEat: You think Winnie murdered Scott.

PainAuChoCOLEat: And blinded her best friend.

ShesGottaGavlt: you assume that the person who hacked the pages is also killing people

PainAuChoCOLEat: It isn't a big leap to make.

PainAuChoCOLEat: And would it be possible for you to muster up a little bit of concern?

PainAuChoCOLEat: Because this is on you, too.

PainAuChoCOLEat: We did those wiki pages together.

PainAuChoCOLEat: If something happens, you're in trouble, same as me.

ShesGottaGavlt: no one is getting in trouble

ShesGottaGavlt: no one has done anything

PainAuChoCOLEat: Tell that to Scott and Andrea.

PainAuChoCOLEat: Tell that to whoever Josh draws a bead on next.

ShesGottaGavlt: so you think josh is a killer

PainAuChoCOLEat: His life is falling apart.

PainAuChoCOLEat: He threatened Andrea and Scott.

PainAuChoCOLEat: Just like he did to Drick today.

PainAuChoCOLEat: He could be next.

PainAuChoCOLEat: Someone has to warn him.

ShesGottaGavlt: please

ShesGottaGavlt: please let me be there when you tell our history teacher that he is on a hit list

ShesGottaGavlt: drawn up by a disgraced high school jock

PainAuChoCOLEat: Then meet me at his class before first period.

PainAuChoCOLEat: Because I'm telling him.

Cole signed off before Gavin could change his mind. He let the decision wash over him. It felt good to be taking action, even if he wasn't sure it was the right action to take. For all he knew, the things that had happened to Scott and Andrea were crazy accidents. For all he knew, whoever had hacked his account was just playing a prank on him. For all he knew, Josh had not turned into a bloodthirsty maniac.

But the only harm in saying something was in being wrong and looking like a fool. The harm in keeping quiet and hoping for the best was that he was right after all.

The real harm was someone else dying.

So why wait until tomorrow? Why not get Drick on the horn and let him know this minute?

Cole hunted the Internet for Drick's number, and found it. But when he called, he got only a busy signal. Over and over again. The man only had a landline. No voice mail. Maybe he took it off the hook at night so he could sleep undisturbed.

Winnie would be up.

Cole dialed her without hesitation. If he couldn't tell Drick, he'd tell her. She needed to know she could be in danger, too. His cell flung out a tether to connect to hers as he devised his speech.

Hi, Winnie. It's me. Cole. Your ex-boyfriend. Cole Redeker. The one you called clingy? Yeah, hi. Listen, there's something I need to tell you. No, I don't like Josh. Yes, I know I've made that abundantly clear already. Yes, in fact, I do think you'd be better off with me. Because I think your current boyfriend killed his best friend, tried to kill your best friend, and might kill our teacher. Don't hate me, I'm trying to save you. Hello? Winnie, are you there?

The ringing stopped. "Hello," said Winnie.

Cole's mouth hung open. His fears for her dangled from his lips.

"What do you want, Cole?"

To take it all back. To fix it. To possess whatever it was she thought he lacked, whatever it was she'd found with Josh.

"This is creepy. I'm hanging up."

"Winnie, wait."

"Good night, Cole."

The phone clicked and she was gone. When he tried calling back, he was sent straight to voice mail. She'd turned off her phone. She'd had enough.

So had Cole. Tomorrow he'd wake up early, track Drick down, and tell him everything in person.

Tomorrow it was all coming out. Tomorrow it would all be over.

Not for Cole, though.

For someone else.

CHAPTER 18

*T*he sun had not yet come up when Arnold Drick arrived for work, and by then he'd already been awake for three hours, his house the snoozy neighborhood's single source of light. After doing his calisthenics, showering, and selecting today's tweed, he reorganized his spice rack (by geographical area of origin), ate his oatmeal, brewed his tea, drank his tea, cleaned his tea kettle and cup, stared out the window, shook his head at the cracked sidewalk, muttered at the neighbor boy's sled left daring to protrude over the property line onto his muddy lawn, wrote a nasty note to said neighbor boy, then tore it up and threw it away, finally removing his glasses to rub the bridge of his nose, weary already. Finally, finally it was a reasonable enough hour to depart for the high school. It was five in the morning.

A few other cars were buoyed in the faculty parking lot, but for now the high school was largely deserted. He cherished the lonely predawn hours when hallways were left unlit, swallowed up in darkness, and the only sounds were those of his footfalls on the fawn-colored carpet or the coo of his red Sharpie on tests and essays. School held its greatest potential for learning when it was empty, and none at all after it was filled with students, when the staff set aside teaching for crowd control.

Arnold Drick was the exception.

He was not a peacekeeper. He was an educator, and would remain so until he breathed his last — much to the disappointment of the department chair. "Florida is nice come the winter," his boss would say. "Heck, it's nice any time of year, really. Like now." But even a casual observer could see that retirement wasn't in the cards for Arnold. Just look at his workspace. There were no family photos tacked to the felt walls of his cubicle, no grandchildren anxiously awaiting his visits. No cruise brochures, no calendar counting down the days to his escape from employment. Nothing to distract him. Nothing else to which he wished to devote his time. He had no reason to give up teaching, and one very good reason to cling to it.

Kids were stupid, and getting stupider.

The evidence was plain to see.

"Just examine the quality of their work," he told the emergency faculty meeting called in the wake of Scott Dare's death. "I can't be the only one who's noticed this degradation. It's rife with shortcuts and stopgaps. It lacks form and critical thought. They slouch their way through their education just like they slouch in and out of class."

"Not to mention the way they dress," snickered a rookie whose misshapen sideburns resembled smeared greasepaint. "All those untucked shirts and bare knees!"

Arnold laughed gamely along with his younger colleagues. Every school's staff was a cast, and each teacher had a role. Arnold was the designated fuddy-duddy, and deemed perfect for the part: a crotchety, rumpled sexagenarian, prone to cogitating and surprise spittle, with plainly visible ear hair a plus. It did no good to fight the label. So he embraced it.

"Their clothes are as indicative of their contempt for schooling as their overreliance on computers to aid their studies," he said, and proceeded to suggest mandatory school uniforms, only to be shouted down.

"We aren't here to discuss dress-code policy," said the principal. "I want to outline the plan for ongoing grief management in wake of the tragedy that claimed Scott Dare's life. . . ."

And what precious little that life amounted to, Arnold tsked as he neared the offices of the history department. Scott was affable enough, if settled and lumpen, a beanbag chair in the form of a student. The administration had struggled to provide enough content to fill the Day of Grieving or the Time for Mourning that followed, to say nothing of the Week of Remembrance through which the school community now slogged. Arnold wondered how he might avoid twiddling his thumbs during the Celebration of Life in just a few days' time, where photo essays and speeches on Scott's love of soccer and board-shorted summers on the Cape would smother any reflection on his other, less estimable qualities, like his utter lack of curiosity or baffling array of baseball caps. Arnold was sure he'd never seen the young man wear the same hat twice.

It seemed to Arnold that Scott had done little of note in his life but die. When the most interesting part of a person's time on earth is the nature of its end, you know you've got problems.

Especially when that end is murder.

This was plain to Arnold well before the brouhaha in the cafeteria instigated by the flat-faced if comely television news reporter. An air pump? To the neck? To be sure, the boy was an idiot, but not so big an idiot that he'd accidentally turn himself into a blimp. Suicide was equally preposterous, and when the police came around with their questions, he told them so.

"Scott Dare simply had too much self-regard to end his own life," Arnold resolved to the gum-chewing detectives, "and too little self-awareness to do it with such grotesque poetry." The detectives had then shot each other a sidelong glance. *Crackpot.*

But the coroner's report proved him right, as he knew it would. His student had been murdered and, as evidenced by the bumbling suburban detectives' obtuse questioning, the identification of a suspect was far off, to say nothing of an arrest.

Arnold had ideas, though.

Ideas that might break the investigation wide open.

If he was ever paid more than a speck of attention.

But no one wanted to listen to old Arnold Drick, did they? Not his students in class, not the police taking his statement, not the checkout girl at the supermarket who insisted his prunes were ten cents more expensive than advertised, and certainly not the cable service helpline who told him he'd fix his signal by resetting the box even though he'd already done that, thank you very much!

Kids were getting stupider. People all over were getting stupider. But not Arnold Drick. He was sharp as a switch and getting sharper, by God. He'd show them, once he cracked this case —

The door to the history department's offices was ajar. A soft, spectral light pooled beneath it, sprung from within the room beyond. Someone was inside. But none of Arnold's colleagues ever beat him to work. He pressed open the door and entered.

In the back of the space, from behind a corner cubicle, a flashlight's halo shone up at the ceiling. It provided just enough light to help Arnold's watery eyes spy a ripple of movement. With it came the hush of rustled papers, and the familiar double squeak of a desk drawer opening and closing. He was in and out of that drawer all day, taking and replacing red pens, red markers, red pencils. He'd asked the custodial staff months ago to oil the drawer. He thought they hadn't listened, but didn't mind being wrong once in a while. Arnold rounded into his cubicle.

"Perhaps you'll have an easier time oiling the drawer with more light. No need to make your work harder."

But the person inside his cubicle was doing work of a different sort. Arnold's computer was on. His grading program was open in a window half hidden by his e-mail program, blinking with a new message.

"You're early," said the intruder, who wore baggy pants and a sweatshirt, hood draped low, concealing the face. Not in evidence was the custodian's jumpsuit, nor the telltale jangle of hundreds of keys slapping thigh.

"And you're no custodian."

The intruder held a fistful of red pens and Sharpies and uncapped one. "Very astute of you." Even in the low light Arnold could tell that something was amiss with the writing implement. Where there ought to have been a tip soaked with red ink was something else. Something pointy and lethal. Something that glinted.

A blade.

The intruder took a step forward, raising the pen/knife high and swinging it down in a long arc, aimed at Arnold's jugular.

Arnold lifted his briefcase with both hands just in time to shield himself from the blade. It dug into the leather hide and lodged there like a squatter. The force of the blow sent Arnold reeling backward, and his attacker with him. The briefcase bounced and unlocked, splaying essays and tests into the air. Toppling over, Arnold found himself wondering how much a leatherworker would charge to repair the puncture to his beloved briefcase, a gift from himself to himself upon the twentieth anniversary of his first day as a teacher. *Too much,* he thought. Then he wondered something else. *Am I about to die?*

Arnold extended his arm to break his fall. The fall broke his arm instead. He knew it the instant he heard the pop, not unlike the sound of breaking Bubble Wrap. Pain followed immediately, and with it, nausea. He hadn't thrown up in decades. *Streak over,* he thought as his stomach revolted and its contents surged like an angry mob. There was a moment, mid-puke, when he felt sorry for his assailant, who caught the worst of it. *What if that sweatshirt is a prized possession? Does vomit come out in the wash?* Then Arnold remembered. *This person just tried to stab me.*

Arnold clambered dizzily to his knees and then up to his feet, cradling his mangled arm close to his body. The attacker lay facedown on the floor nearby, down but not out, clutching ribs and groaning while Arnold steadied himself on the edge of a desk. What now? Press his advantage? Call the police? Run like the dickens? The moment's indecision was enough to grant his attacker a second wind. Arnold lumbered down the walk space between the two rows of cubicles, bumping against the partitions as he made for the door. Behind him came the sound of his would-be killer scrambling on hands and knees, scuttling after him like vermin.

Each labored step took Arnold closer to the door, but did it matter? His pursuer was younger by far, stronger — and gaining ground.

And perhaps re-armed.

Arnold dared not find out. Already injured, he would not survive another encounter with that blade. But nor would he win a footrace to safety. Arnold was doomed, whether he made it out the door or not. He could only survive if he was granted mercy — or with help from others.

Beside the door, just steps away, was a red fire alarm.

Arnold's only shot at salvation.

Get to the door.

Pull the alarm.

Pull it and the early arrivals will be alerted.

Pull it and the maniac chasing you will have no choice but to take flight.

Pull it!

Arnold reached, trigger at the cusp of his fingertips — and then not.

The floor gave out.

Arnold looked down just in time to see his foot had landed on one of the assignments coughed up from his briefcase. It slipped out from beneath him, along with his legs, and for a moment he was weightless in midair, bicycling his limbs like a hapless cartoon carnivore, outwitted again. Arnold belly flopped, his head whiplashing to the ground, snapping his jaw. His breath evacuated in a gust, his lungs crumpling inside him. The assignment on which he slipped fluttered to his side, but the fire alarm remained fixed on the wall above him. He lifted his good arm toward it, even though he knew. There would be no help from others. As for mercy . . .

The hooded figure appeared above him, pen/knife in hand, and retrieved the paper. "Oh, look." *That voice.* "A B-minus."

Something about that voice. "Tough break for . . . Cole Redeker." It wasn't right. "You're not an easy grader, are you, Mr. Drick?" It was familiar. But it didn't belong. "But you're not doing the grading now, are you?" The hood came off. "I am." That face. "You didn't prepare for this assignment, did you, Mr. Drick?" He knew that face. "Sloppy work. I'm afraid I'll have to grade accordingly." The pen/knife went up in the air, and came back down at his face. Into his broken, gaping mouth.

People were getting stupider, Arnold thought as he was stabbed again and again, his mouth brimming with blood, flooding his airway, *and he was stupid, too.* The answers were there in front of him all along. He should have known this was coming. He should have figured it out. He could have stopped it. He could have saved himself. And others, too. But he was too late. His teaching days were over. He would be dead in moments. And not long after, others would be dead, too.

Cole hitched a ride with his dad and arrived at school an hour before class began. He went straight to Drick's classroom. Drick wasn't there, but Gavin was. "Talk to him yet?"

"I thought he'd be here. You haven't seen him?"

Gavin's face crinkled. "Isn't he, like, up with the farmers?"

It was weird, Cole thought. "Maybe he's out today. Think we got a sub?"

"Rise and shine, Cole. Dreamtime is over. You sent him an e-mail last night, right? Did you get a read receipt?"

"I didn't check."

"So let's go find out."

They forgot all about Drick's computer when they found Drick. Arriving at the history department, they saw a rust-colored stain streaking from the door down the aisle and ending at his desk. Someone stood there, between them and the desk chair, hunched.

"Hello?"

Chetley turned, his face the color of dull concrete, his hands gloved red.

"He was like this when I came in. I swear. I tried to save him. But he was already gone."

Drick's body was slumped in his chair. Cole wondered why he was wearing a bib. Then he realized it wasn't a bib. It was blood. Congealing blood coated the front of his shirt and jacket. His head rolled to one side with the added weight of the foreign objects clustered together, protruding from his mouth, broken wide open.

Red pens.

Red pencils.

Red Sharpies.

And everywhere there were papers. Assignments and essays and tests and reports. All labeled with a giant red grade, the same red grade that was carved into Drick's forehead.

F.

Arnold Drick

From *Wikipedia*, the free encyclopedia

Arnold Drick is an **American** teacher of **history**. He received a bachelor's degree in history from **Amherst** and a Master of Arts in teaching from **Brown**. During his career as an educator at Springfield High School he failed on average five students every year. His fickle method of grading contributed to countless others not receiving admission to their college of choice.

He lived by the red pen, and he died by it, too.

CHAPTER 19

By the time the police arrived on the scene of Drick's murder, Cole and Gavin had been removed to the corridor, ordered out by the principal. Cole wanted to haul ass as far away as possible, even if that only meant going to first-period physics. But school went into lockdown as soon as 9-1-1 was called. Classes were canceled before they'd even begun. Gavin and Cole were the only students in the building, anyway, and Gavin wasn't going anywhere, not until Spring Showers showed up. He was intent on getting on camera.

"Wipe that disgusted look off your face," he told Cole. "Like it or not, we're headline news. 'Hottie Heroes Happen on History Homicide!' 'Kids Catch Killer, Crowned Kings of Community!'"

Cole surfaced from shock. "We don't know Chetley killed Drick."

"Maybe you're confused about the meaning of getting 'caught red-handed.' It has nothing to do with what happens when your mother interrupts your me-time."

"But what possible reason would Chetley have to do something like that?" The question had plagued Cole since the moment they'd happened on the gruesome scene. "Why would he kill Drick? And Scott? And go after Andrea? What does he get out of any of it? It makes no sense!"

"Let the police make sense out of it. Our job is just to tell them what we found when we got here."

"And about the Wikipedia pages," Cole reminded him.

Gavin hurled a look at Cole. "I honestly don't know how you got to be at the top of the class with that brain of yours. If we mention anything about Wikipedia, we'll be bunking with Chetley in jail."

"I thought you said we were heroes."

"We are!" Gavin lowered his voice. "But that will be over as soon as it gets out we drew up a list of people we might like to see dead, then went and posted it online for the world to see. Because ha-ha, aren't we funny? Too bad psycho Chetley didn't get the joke and took it upon himself to carry out our wishes."

"We didn't actually want them dead, though!" Cole protested. His head pounded. "Not really."

"Who is going to believe us, Cole? The truth about the pages comes out and we're automatically linked to someone who killed a bright shiny star athlete and an old coot. At best the cops think we're accomplices. At worst we're the masterminds. And while I'm honored when you call me a mad genius, I'd prefer not to hear it from the district attorney at a press conference announcing my arrest!"

He had a point.

So Cole resolved to tell the police nothing about the Wikipedia entries, and nothing to suggest Drick's death was connected to Scott's, or to Andrea's freak accident. Gavin and Cole ironed out a script, and when the detective finally came to interview them, they stuck to it. The detective thanked them for their help and instructed them not to discuss what they'd seen with anyone, especially the news media.

They regrouped at Benito's.

"One good thing about Drick meeting his doom," Gavin pronounced, mozzarella garlanded from his mouth, "his curve dies with him." He slurped up the remaining cheese, the last of a pizza bianca, and raised a foamy mug of root beer to his lips. "To Bs of all varieties: We hardly knew ye."

Cole couldn't even think about celebrating. His head was sloppy with images he might never be rid of.

Chetley falling to his knees and humping toward them, whimpering his innocence.

The police hauling him away, arms pinned back, cuffs tinkling a tuneless melody.

Drick's remains sewn up into a body bag. The zipper snagging on a gnarled thread, refusing to budge.

Drick's remains.

Drick's remains.

Drick's remains.

"A guy died," Cole croaked. "Just hours ago. And you're already reaping the benefits."

Gavin dabbed a napkin at the corners of his mouth. "I'd call it 'taking comfort,' but that's the difference between you and me. Me: glass half full."

"Me: glass half empty?"

"No, you: glass smashed to bits."

Cole would never have described Gavin as the sensitive type. But his attitude now was callous, even for him. "Doesn't it bother you? One day he was our history teacher. The next day he isn't. He's nothing. Gone. Just lesson plans and a lanyard. A corpse."

Gavin looked down at his pizza as though he might divine an answer in its crust. He looked back up at Cole. Something was different in his eyes. "Of course it bothers me," he said, without a trace of amusement. "I just don't know what you want me to do about it. I'm not going to cry. I'm not going to get dramatic. It's not like Drick was my father."

"You hate your father."

"Correction: I am over my father," Gavin said. He was also over Cole's bellyaching. "I reserve my hate for others. You, on the other hand, did hate Scott. The guy was your friend, once upon a time. But I don't remember you throwing yourself on his coffin after he got hosed. You didn't even go to his service."

Cole shut up.

"Exactly. Are you gonna finish that?"

Cole sat back, abandoning his untouched pizza. Gavin was wrong. Cole had gone to the service. Well, he tried, anyway. He just hadn't gone inside. He'd dressed in a plain white shirt and a tie, as soberly as his wardrobe allowed, and walked to the church by himself only to stop a block away. Scott's parents stood outside receiving mourners, and Cole was seized by a new, unsavory terror.

The terror of not knowing what to say.

We were good friends and I'll miss him was a half-truth.

I think I may have inadvertently caused his death was inappropriate, to say the least, and not necessarily true.

Cole could have just said *I'm very sorry for your loss*, but by the time that had occurred to him he was already blocks away and committed to mourning Scott in his own private way. He kept on walking until he was home, his shame trotting alongside him like a stray dog he'd made the mistake of feeding once, now bonded to him for life.

Gavin hadn't gone to the service, either, but he didn't seem to feel bad about it, or even care that he didn't feel bad about it. Cole wasn't sure if he envied Gavin or was disgusted by him.

"You make it sound like I wanted Scott to die," Cole said.

Gavin lowered his voice and looked deeply at Cole. "No, I don't. But if that's what you actually hear in that messed-up head of yours, I'll change my tune. Because neither one of us can afford to sound like we wanted anyone to die. So just keep your mouth shut, okay? We did the right thing." He finally seemed to grasp that his lighthearted policy of laughing in the face of violent murder didn't help Cole remain calm. "Chetley's caught, Josh is off the hook, and Winnie is safe. It's too bad about Drick. I wish he hadn't died. I really do. But there's nothing to be gained by telling the cops the truth."

"Did you recognize the detective? I think he was the same one we saw at Andrea's, when I went to deliver her cookies. What if he's picked up on the Wikipedia entries? What if he's onto us?"

"Then he might have asked us questions that probed deeper than, 'Was Mr. Drick chill?' and 'Did he and Chetley have beef?' Taylor Swift was asked tougher questions in the last issue of *Teen Vogue*."

Cole's eyes narrowed. It sounded like a joke, but at the same time, it didn't. "Since when do you read *Teen Vogue*?"

Gavin actually reddened. "Just for the quizzes. Guess what, Harry Styles is my 1D love match."

Cole pushed back from the table. "I'm not sure about this."

"You're telling me. I've wasted years crushing on Louis."

"I mean about Drick. Scott. Andrea. The Wikis. Keeping quiet about all of it," Cole said. "If we come forward now, we're responsible citizens who want to aid the investigation. If we say nothing, we run the risk of looking like we have something to hide when someone figures it out and comes forward for us."

"Like who?"

Cole was about to remind Gavin that someone was already close to doing that when she sat down at the table and did the reminding for him.

"Guten Abend, Jungs," breezed Lila as she dropped into the booth next to startled, frozen Cole. Today's ensemble featured bright red jeans, suspenders over a crisp white shirt, and a green Alpine hat, tilted at a jaunty angle.

"Well, if it isn't Miss Hipster Oktoberfest," Gavin drawled. "Tell me something, why do you dress the way you do?"

"To give people who have nothing to say something to talk about." She'd answered this question before. "I think the real question is, why don't *you* dress the way I do? Some lederhosen and short pants would really make those chicken legs pop." She faced Cole. "Scooch over, will you?" He could feel her breath on his face. "Or don't. I can do up close and personal." Cole hopped his butt toward the wall, trapped. Gavin slid out, ignoring Cole's silent pleas for rescue.

"That's my cue. Toodle-loo, Cole. You too, Heidi."

Lila reached for the pizza. "Gonna eat that?" She didn't wait for him to wave her on. "Thanks. I'm famished. Chasing down a red-hot story all day long sure does burn calories. I hear you and Gavin had an even longer day."

Cole wasn't going there. "I don't know what you're talking about."

Lila sighed. "Are you really going to shrink from me like I have cooties and pretend you and Gavin did not just this morning happen upon the gruesome death of SHS's most notorious grader? Because a certain chatty Cathy on the custodial staff puts you on the scene."

What point was there in denying it? "The police told us not to say anything about it."

"The police can *ask* you not to say anything about it, but they can't *order* you not to say anything about it."

"Well, they asked nicely. And my parents raised a polite boy. So if you're asking for my comment, I can't give you any. Now if you'll excuse me . . ." Lila made no move to get out of Cole's way. "I will climb over you if I have to."

"A polite boy like you? I think not. I think you're going to agree to give me an exclusive instead."

"And if I don't?" Cole was done. Enough. He'd cowed to Gavin, been toyed with by Winnie, and been manhandled by Josh and Scott. He refused to let Lila push him around, too — even if a small but growing part of him kind of liked it. "You'll cobble together a story with your other sources with or without my quotes. You'll put Gavin and me on the scene and mess with the police investigation. The cops will get pissed, want to know who the heck this Walda Winchell person is, and I'll be happy to give them your number."

Lila coiled a string of cheese around her finger. "You could do all that. And when they come to me I'll blow their investigation wide open by pointing out the Wiki pages they've yet to notice." Cole stopped cold. "I imagine they'll be pretty keen on tracking down whoever created those pages. I imagine they'll be even keener to do so when they realize there are other

124

still-living members of the SHS community who happen to have strange deaths foretold on their Wikipedia profiles."

Cole was glad he hadn't eaten anything. If he had, he'd have barfed it all up right then. "What other pages?" was all he could muster in response.

"Tomorrow night. You. Me. Schnitzel. The Blue Danube in Hartford at seven p.m. We'll talk all about Drick, Andrea, Scott, the Wiki pages . . . and whatever else we can think of." Cole realized he needn't have eaten anything to get the dry heaves. "Don't look so down, Cole. The food's great and I'm good company. I promise. Are we agreed?"

Cole swallowed. "Fine."

Lila flashed a starry smile.

"Good," she said. "It's a date."

CHAPTER 20

A succession of texts early the next morning insisted Cole open his eyes well before he was accustomed.

But this was not a rude awakening by any means. Cole welcomed the relief from his dreams. He couldn't remember them specifically. Just moments after regaining consciousness they were already vanishing, sucked out of sight like an unlucky animal swallowed in quicksand. Cole knew by the thrum of his heartbeat that these dreams were bad. That was all he needed to know.

He reached for his phone, but paused. Maybe the texts were from Lila. Maybe she was in touch with special instructions. Maybe she wasn't kidding about that lederhosen stuff. Or maybe she had to cancel their plans — their *date*, and no, her choice of words was not lost on him. But would Lila postpone dinner with a text, or tell him in person, the better to make him squirm? And did he really want her to cancel? Good schnitzel was surprisingly difficult to come by this side of the Alps.

And then there was Lila. She probably wasn't the worst person to spend time with. Bizarre, sure. Baffling, most definitely. But beyond the German affectation and the habit for daily transforming her look like a gamer always bored with his avatar, she had a quirky, spirited appeal. And when Cole was with her, he was on his toes. There were worse ways to be.

Another text rolled in. Cole was thinking too hard. And

about the wrong girl. Winnie was the goal. He took his phone with the resignation of the damned.

Gavin
wake up
check it out
spring showers on twitter
chetley released
to trade places with your nemesis
time to saddle up whinny
unless you have better things to do
german things

Cole tumbled out of bed, springing for his laptop. In his haste he failed to fully detach foot from sheet and fell over, greeting the floor with his forehead. Cursing the pain, he dialed Gavin while stoking the computer to life.

"What happened?" asked Cole.

"I told you, read Twitter."

Cole called up the website and added Spring Showers to his feed.

Winnie Hoffman @WinWin100
@ABrindleDocent where's the "report abuse" button
5 minutes ago   Favorite Retweet Reply

Rabid Doc Lenten @ABrindleDocent
@WinWin100 @OTruffleShuffle oooooooh
somebody is in trouuubleee #SHS
11 minutes ago   Favorite Retweet Reply

Spring Showers @2WSPG_Spring

@ABrindleDocent Look for a student? #SHS

12 minutes ago   Favorite Retweet Reply

Rabid Doc Lenten @ABrindleDocent.

@2WSPG_Spring enquiring minds want to know #SHS

14 minutes ago   Favorite Retweet Reply

Rabid Doc Lenten @ABrindleDocent

@2WSPG_Spring what person of interest #SHS

15 minutes ago   Favorite Retweet Reply

Spring Showers @2WSPG_Spring

Person of interest sought for questioning? #SHS

18 minutes ago   Favorite Retweet Reply

Spring Showers @2WSPG_Spring

Police don't lack for suspect? #SHS

20 minutes ago   Favorite Retweet Reply

Spring Showers @2WSPG_Spring

Sources say #SHS teacher freed, cleared of
colleague's murder?

20 minutes ago   Favorite Retweet Reply

Cole's fingers streaked across the keyboard.

Cole_Redeker @PainAuChoCOLEat

@ABrindleDocent not cool

26 seconds ago   Favorite Retweet Reply

"Wow, look at Spring Showers go! Who knew our hometown girl had a future laying local-Emmy bait back when she was campaigning for Miss Springfield in her bikini?"

"Who is this ABrindleDocent and why are they harassing Winnie?"

"Who cares?" asked Gavin.

Cole had seen that Twitter handle before, issuing condolences in the wake of Andrea's accident. Whoever was the force behind "Rabid Doc Lenten" had given up asking about Andrea's condition to troll Josh and Winnie. Cole made a mental note to scroll through the Tweeter's history later. Right now he had his work cut out for him deciphering Spring Showers's broadcast. "Everything this lady writes ends with a question mark. Is she reporting news or asking us if there's news to report?"

"I think we'll find out come first period?" Gavin chortled and hung up.

Cole dressed in a stupor, his mind thudding from the headache and questions combined.

Chetley, released? Josh, targeted? Winnie, single? School, on?

"What did you expect, another week of memorializing?" Gavin asked when they later met at Cole's locker. "The district only has so many snow days to play with, and it burned a couple so we could grieve for Scott. We can't afford to blow any more on a geezer teacher nobody will remember come next fall." There was sarcasm in Gavin's voice, but Cole knew he wasn't far from the truth. "Who dressed you this morning? You're all misbuttoned."

First period commenced. Little was learned. Lesson plans were mailed in. Few spoke, and fewer listened. Cole had never heard the school so quiet, and just the morning before he'd been one of only a handful of people inside it. Students and teachers alike drifted blankly from one classroom to the next as if standing on moving sidewalks. Minutes ticked by and Cole's pulse gradually quickened. A kind of dread wormed through his insides, gnawing at his guts. He didn't know where the feeling came from until he realized where he was headed next.

History.

A prim, dusty woman stood in the entry, recognized by Cole as a standby substitute. She welcomed each student to class with a timid smile. Cole headed for his seat, skirting Drick's desk. The dead teacher's trademark rubber-banded bundle of red pens and dog-eared textbook still sat there, a gravestone, impossible to disregard. Cole sat down and waited as classmates filed in. He watched the door. Through it came Winnie.

Her eyes were shadowed, but not with makeup — this was the natural result of little sleep. Her face was pinched and washed out, drawn with just a few tints of pale. Her hair normally swung around in a wide swathe, a thick brown veil. But today it was controlled, swept up in an artful tangle and pinned behind her head. Her expression was blank. She could have been in shock or deep concentration or on automatic pilot.

She was beautiful.

Winnie took her seat and let her bag plop to the floor. It slumped and a few papers slipped out. She didn't notice, and Cole suddenly found himself at her feet, collecting them.

"Oh. Thanks," said Winnie, surfacing.

"No problem." Cole set the papers down on her desk. On top was a calculus test. There was no mistaking the three-digit score at the top, a smiley face in number form. She'd aced it.

Cole had received the second B of his life two periods before in English, for subpar work comparing and contrasting *The Count of Monte Cristo* with its modern-day successors. The assignment should've been a cakewalk. Any assignment should've been a cakewalk. But his grades had taken a backseat to his real-life story of revenge, death, and destruction. From the looks of Winnie's test, she was handling the stress just fine. Her 105 percent (couldn't she pass up the extra credit question just once?) was bad juju for Cole's valedictory prospects.

But so what if Winnie's grades were stable and Cole's were bottoming out? Scott was dead. Drick was dead. Fretting over Cole's place in the class standings felt vulgar, like wondering what kind of food was served at a wake. Winnie discreetly turned over her test, but Cole had the nagging sense that she was pleased he'd seen it.

"This is weird, right?" *Articulate as ever, Cole.* "I mean, Drick. Gone."

Winnie agreed. "It'd be one thing if he'd had a heart attack. But to go the way he did . . ." She broke off and looked away, shaking her head.

Her shoulder faced Cole.

It begged to be touched.

"Are you okay?" he asked. She didn't answer.

He began to lower into a crouch, prepared to combat her tears with a steady hand and the Ryan Gosling eyes he'd practiced for just this moment. *Hey, girl,* they'd purr, *just letting you know you can talk to me.* But when Winnie turned back to him her eyes were dry. There was no trace of vulnerability. Just confusion.

"What are you doing?"

Abort!

"Just tying my shoe." He looked down. It was tied just fine. "Retying it, I mean. Loose laces make for crooked faces." Cole flash-fried embarrassment. Above him Winnie seemed not to notice. She inhaled, exhaled deeply, and redirected the conversation back at herself.

"I'm fine. Distracted, that's all. Busy. Constantly studying. Extracurriculars all the time. Tennis. They don't hand you valedictorian just because you want it."

Cole stood up, wobbling. "Yeah." Wasn't she forgetting something? "Plus all the stuff with Andrea. And, you know. A couple of murders here at school. That stuff has to take a toll. Right?"

Winnie shifted uncomfortably, almost as though it hadn't occurred to her. "Definitely. I just talked to Andrea yesterday."

"How is she?"

Winnie cocked her head. "How do you think?"

"I mean." Cole didn't know how to say it, and quickly browsed his options for a smooth exit from this dead-end topic.

"You mean, what? How does she look?"

Too slow. "I guess. It's none of my business. I only asked . . . you know. Because."

"Because what?"

Because you know why, Winnie. She was not just proficient at Arabic, Mandarin, and English; for all her pretend ignorance, Winnie was fluent in Cole, too. She knew his signals. He'd been sending them in glaring, increasingly desperate waves since the day of their breakup. She just wanted him to put into words what he'd only been able to say with longing looks. Right?

Cole opened his mouth and shut it. From nowhere an image

of Lila had sprouted in his head. Looking down at him as she tenderly cradled his head, throbbing after she'd clocked him with her serve. He weeded out the image of Lila and opened his mouth again.

"Because she's your friend. You care about her." Two short sentences and somehow he'd run out of air. Cole drew another breath. "And what you care about, I care about. Because I care about you."

It came out like a word problem, and with less conviction than he'd heard it in his head. But he forgave himself. Cole's romance was rusty, and Lila's intrusion into his thoughts had thrown him off his game. Winnie's response would decide whether he'd have a chance to iron out the kinks.

"That's really nice of you to say, Cole." She might have actually meant it.

"Say what?" came another voice.

Josh's.

Cole was too hopped up on Winnie's attention to notice the stillness that had gripped the room with Josh's entrance. All eyes fell on the predator prowling in their midst. Collectively, breathing slowed and heartbeats picked up. Motes of dust hung frozen in the air as if waiting with everyone else for carnage to ensue.

"Say what," Josh repeated. This time it wasn't a question.

"It's none of your business." The statement hadn't come from Cole.

It came from Winnie.

Josh was as surprised as Cole, and stood there for a moment wearing the stupid expression of a king unfamiliar to dissent.

"What?"

"I said it's none of your business," she said, adding with emphasis, "it's between Cole and me." She turned back to Cole, as if to continue their conversation.

Josh was snubbed.

The sensation was discombobulating. Cole felt like he'd driven over an unexpected rise and been drawn out of his seat and made suddenly, briefly weightless. Josh was even more disoriented. His jaw seemed to come unhinged and fall agape as he worked out what to say in response.

The bell rang. Gavin scooted inside just before the sub closed the door.

"Everyone, please take your seats. The principal will be along any minute now to speak to you all." Cole's classmates shuffled to their desks. Josh didn't move from Winnie's side, and so neither did Cole.

"Let's get out of here," Josh whispered to Winnie in a plaintive, friendless voice. "Meet me at my car and we'll go somewhere. We'll talk."

The sub verged on Drick's desk, moving scrap paper from one side to the other. "Everyone?"

Winnie faced Josh. "She wants you to sit down."

"Gentlemen, we're about to start."

Josh touched Winnie's arm. "That's okay. We're not staying."

A current raced through the classroom, eddying amongst the students. "I'm not going anywhere," said Winnie. "Especially not with you."

Cole's classmates were looking up from their books, giving up the pretense that they were not, in fact, hanging on every word. Josh hooked his fingers under Winnie's elbow.

"It'll be okay. I promise. Just come with me."

What happened next became the stuff of legend. Cole would remember none of it. That can happen when you get a concussion, which is what Cole got. Accounts of the events that unfolded varied sensationally by the IQ and excitability of the witness, but a more-or-less reliable narrative emerged and was recorded for posterity by the *Muckraker*. Lila made quick work of the story. The SHS student body got the news in a mass text.

...NEWS FLASH...Cole Redeker defends honor of Winnie Hoffman from rumored serial killer Josh Truffle...

A free-for-all ensued today in the honors history class of the late teacher Arnold Drick when disgraced former soccer star/knuckle dragger Josh Truffle attempted to spirit Winnie Hoffman from school against her will. Standing in the way was none other than Cole Redeker, better known for his biscuits than acts of bravery.

This latest episode can only serve to further damage Truffle's once-golden reputation, already marred by a violent confrontation with his formerly animate best friend, Scott Dare, as well as a threat of bodily harm to the notorious Mr. Drick. According to witnesses on the scene, Truffle entered the history class shortly before the beginning of seventh period and approached the desk of Hoffman, his estranged girlfriend. He found Hoffman already deep in conversation with Redeker — the ex-boyfriend she'd dumped in order to date Truffle — and flew into a rage.

"It had to be, like, the biggest thing to hit history since I don't know what," commented the contextually challenged senior Katrina van der Smeenk. Visibly shaken by the ruckus, van der Smeenk claims Truffle demanded Hoffman go with her. "She started screaming at him, 'Eff you, eff you, why would I go anywhere with a murderer?' It got crazy after that."

Other witnesses dispute van der Smeenk's recollection, but all agree that a distraught Truffle pleaded with Hoffman to leave class with him, despite her continued refusals.

That's when Redeker stepped in.

"Cole wouldn't stand for it," said Redeker's sidekick, Gavin Peters. "You don't mess with the lesser sex in his presence. He's old-school!" Peters says Redeker intervened to prevent Truffle's manhandling of Hoffman. "He told Josh, 'Hands off the lady.' And Josh was all, 'What if I don't, brah?!' And Cole rolled up his sleeves and said, 'I'm not your brah, *son*,'" (Editor's note: Emphasis is Peters's).

Redeker then endeavored to release Hoffman from Truffle's grip, resulting in much adolescent pushing and shoving. Substitute teacher Mrs. Millicent Purdue fluttered around the fray but was unable to bring the altercation to a halt, and departed to seek help as punches were finally thrown, which culminated in Redeker taking a right hook to the head and dropping to the floor, out cold.

By the time Principal Trusk arrived on the scene, Truffle had departed, though not with Hoffman. She stayed at Cole's side as the school nurse arrived and removed him to her office for care and observation.

Truffle was seen tearing out of the SHS student parking lot in his BMW. It is believed he is wanted for questioning by the police.

His whereabouts are unknown.

CHAPTER 21

Cole awoke for the second time in twelve hours, but for the first time ever in the nurse's office. The light above his curtained-off section of the exam room was dimmed, but there was enough fluorescent spillage from the surrounding beds that he could clearly make out an eye chart and a poster advertising the benefits of hooking up.

Something about that didn't seem right.

His head felt airy, as if everything inside had settled to the bottom of his skull, like the contents of a box of cereal left too long on a store shelf. He tried to sit up, but this morning's breakfast gushed discontentedly in his stomach, so he hiked back onto his elbows instead.

"You're up."

Cole's head flopped to the other side. A girl sat in a chair beside him. She had a lot of hair. He knew her. He knew her very well. Or used to. Or never did.

"Whitney. Hi."

The girl in the chair with the stare-worthy hair smiled. "No. Not Whitney. Winnie."

"Right," said Cole. "Whitney." No, not right. "I mean, Whitney."

Everything was coming out wrong.

"Here." She stood up and rushed to his side. "Put your head

back down," she said, helping him. She was his nurse, but not the nurse.

Cole closed his eyes. "It hurts to think."

"Then don't try so hard. A doctor is supposed to come to check you out but I heard the nurse say they think you got a concussion. If things are muddy, that's why."

"How'd I get a concussion?"

"How much do you remember?"

The sound of his heart caving in on itself when she dumped him came to mind. Like it was yesterday.

"Class?" he asked.

"Do you remember Josh?"

"As a concept? A person? Or an event?"

"Sounds like you're already bouncing back," she said, redistributing the bangs that fell across his forehead. "He hit you pretty hard. Do you remember why? Do you remember getting in his way? Standing up for me?"

"Vaguely," he answered, though he had the nagging sense that she hadn't exactly deserved it.

"Under normal circumstances that would have pissed me off. I'm quite capable of standing up for myself. But I'm making an exception in your case. Josh actually tried to drag me out like I was his property. Before he took off for parts unknown."

There was something he had to tell her about Josh. He wasn't sure what.

"But then you were there."

It had to do with Cole.

"Standing between us."

Something Cole did.

"I always knew you cared."

Something bad.

"But I didn't know you cared that much."

Something she needed to know about.

"Josh lost it. If Gavin hadn't pulled him off you, it might have been a real beating. Or worse, maybe. I know he's been through a lot. And people are saying all kinds of stuff about him. But I've never seen it. I didn't think he was really capable of those things. It's obvious now something's seriously wrong with him. I feel like such an idiot for never catching on. It's like he has this other side he's kept stowed away, hidden from everybody. A bad side. Something totally . . . I don't know . . ."

Cole remembered. "Wicked."

Her gaze had drifted with thoughts of Josh. Now it refocused on Cole. "Yeah. I guess. Wicked."

Cole pressed his palms against his eyes and rubbed. Could he massage his mind back into coherence? "No. Listen. Wicked. Wickedpedia."

She lifted a shoulder and let it drop, blankly. "I don't understand."

"You need to look at it. Wickedpedia."

"Is that a parody of the website or something?"

"No. Not parity." *Parody! Stupid tongue!* "The real site. You need to read it. Your page."

"I don't have a Wikipedia page."

"You do now. You need to read it. You need to know. And be ready. In case Josh comes around. Whatever you do, don't let him near you."

"Believe me, I won't. I broke up with him."

"I don't want to talk about Josh anymore."

"Me neither," said Winnie. "I just want to kiss you."

She leaned down. Her hair poured over her shoulder and into his mouth. It smelled of eucalyptus and tasted of carcinogen. Cole hacked up the bulk of it and picked out the rest.

"Sorry," she said. "You'd think I'd have this figured out by now." She moved in for a second take.

But instead of welcoming her kiss, this time Cole turned away from it.

"What's wrong?"

Yeah, Cole. What's wrong?

"I thought you wanted to talk," he said. "About us."

"Sure. We can talk." She said it with a look that would have been more at home out to dinner, when presented with an entrée she had not ordered and did not want. "I just thought a kiss would say a lot more with a lot less."

"That would kind of be, like, glossing over a lot of stuff, wouldn't it?" A voice inside Cole shrieked, *Gloss, you fool, gloss! This is what you've been waiting for, isn't it? The easy restoration of your couple status and the free kisses that accompany it!*

"Like what?" she asked.

Cole told the voice to zip it. "Like . . . why you dumped me . . . and why you started going out with Josh two minutes later."

"God." She sat back down. "You really want to get into that?"

Did he? Or was this the concussion talking? Asking a person who hurt you why they hurt you isn't like asking them to point you toward the can. And it isn't like they make it out to be in the movies, or on TV. It may come from a place of anger and sadness, but mostly it's about humiliation. To ask a person what you did to deserve their contempt is to assume that you may have deserved their contempt, Cole thought. It's to assume that you may deserve it again. Cole had to know. He had to hear her explain herself before he could decide whether she'd ever kiss him again. He had to know if she could hurt him again the same way she'd hurt him before.

"Tell me why you did it," he asked.

She bit the inside of her mouth and said nothing. So Cole said something instead, and with each word he spent a little more of the meager self-respect he'd scraped together since she'd dropped him for Josh.

"Did you just not like me enough anymore? Was it because I'm not hot enough? Did I do something? What did I do wrong?"

Winnie looked up at the ceiling. Then down at the floor, like she was scrounging for an answer. But Cole knew Winnie always had an answer for everything. If she couldn't speak now, it was because she didn't want to say it. Because she didn't want to look bad. Because she needed him now and couldn't afford to lose him.

A third voice broke the surface from behind the curtain. "The same thing you're doing right now, Cola. It's unbecoming, the way you throw yourself at her feet. She's not a goddess to be worshipped. She's a girl. And if the gossip I've heard is right, a pretty faithless one. If you don't act like her equal, she'll never treat you like it."

Winnie flung open the curtain. Lying on the next bed was Chetley. He was curled comfily on his side, tuned into their personal business like they were his private soap opera. Except talking to the characters on a TV show never affected the plot. Chetley had been there the whole time, listening in. And with a few choice words he'd altered their course.

"You were listening to us?" she shrieked.

"It's the only entertainment around." Chetley yawned.

"What are you doing in here?" Cole asked.

The nurse bustled in and supplied an answer. "He's gathering his wits. Aren't you, Mr. Chetley," she said with a rude pop, the smack of latex on skin. "Came in to discuss your leave of absence with the principal and broke down into a blubbery mess, didn't you? Right there in the teachers' lounge with the decaf and day-old Danish."

Chetley turned away and drew his knees to his chest.

Clearly school nurses weren't bound to the same rules of patient confidentiality as other medical professionals.

The nurse pointed at Winnie. "You. Out."

"We need to finish talking," Winnie told the nurse.

"He needs to rest. The doctor is on his way."

"FaceTime later?" she asked Cole.

Winnie let the door draw to a close behind her without an answer. A brief quiet fell over the room before the sound of Chetley's paper sheet quibbling with his shifting weight. Cole stared at the blue-green curtain between them for a long time and wondered if Chetley was staring back.

Yup. Alone in the room with a former murder suspect. Nothing school security should be concerned about.

"Gavin and I have this disagreement," Cole said to the curtain. "He thinks the staff here is all wrapped up in what goes on among the students. I say we'd have to be supremely self-absorbed to believe we're of any interest to you. It's not like you all don't have lives of your own."

"You know something? Your friend Gavin is a smart guy. You should really give him more credit. Kid's going places."

Cole stared. The curtain revealed nothing.

"That's pretty sad," Cole ventured.

"Gotta get your kicks somehow."

"So you get yours from students?" Cole asked. He thought of something else. "And other teachers?"

The curtain was unmoved.

"I don't know what you mean."

Cole was taught to respect his elders, teachers especially. Chetley wasn't much of a teacher, but he was still an elder. Barely. Cole figured they were more or less equals. "I mean your colleague. Mr. Drick."

Nothing from the curtain.

"The guy who was stabbed to death?"

Nothing at first. Then Chetley squeezed out, "I know who you mean." He cleared his throat and lowered his voice. "I had his blood on my hands."

"I remember," said Cole. "I also remember the police. They took you away in cuffs. And now you're here."

The curtain undulated, like Chetley had drawn a finger across it.

"Because they realized they had the wrong guy. Josh is the one they want. He killed Scott for taking his spot on the team. He killed Drick for keeping him off it. Poor guy seems to over-react when things don't go his way. He's not likely to be feel too great about his girlfriend dumping him." The curtain's move-ment came to a stop. "Or the guy she dumped him for."

Cole didn't need Chetley to tell him that. He just needed Chetley to tell him one thing.

"What were you doing there? Why were you in the history department's offices?"

Chetley didn't say anything. The silence went on so long that

Cole thought he'd fallen asleep. Cole was on the edge of a doze, himself, when Chetley's voice softly peeked under the curtain.

"I was there because this is where I work, Cole. I was working. Why were you there?"

"I go to class here, Mr. Chetley. Mr. Drick was my teacher. I was going to see my teacher."

"So early? With Gavin?"

"We needed to talk about an assignment."

"Huh," Chetley said. "I suppose that makes sense." His calculated tone told Cole he had a more interesting idea. "More sense than anything to do with his Wikipedia page. Right?"

Cole grabbed the bed for dear life, the paper sheet stiff under his fingers. Where was the nurse? "I don't know what you're talking about."

"Maybe you know it better by 'Wickedpedia.' That's what you called it just now when you spoke to Winnie, right? When you told her to check it out? Her own page?"

"I think you misheard me. That can happen sometimes when you eavesdrop on people."

"Mr. Drick has a page. It was there on his computer screen when I found him. It's not every day that a high school history teacher rates his own Internet reference. But then, there's a Wikipedia page on the Pig Olympics, so why not Arnold Drick? There was something weird about this one, though."

Now would be a good time for the nurse to return. "You're telling me you found a guy dead in this school and you stopped to read his Wikipedia page?"

There was an abrupt crash from beyond the curtain, the brittle crunch of the paper on Chetley's bed. Cole saw his feet touch the floor. "The weird thing about this one was that it described his death to a tee. Don't you think that's weird, Cole? It's like someone knew how Mr. Drick was going to die before he died. Like they planned it and advertised it for everyone to see . . . if anyone cared to look."

Cole couldn't breathe. Does a concussion do that to you? Or massive guilt? "Yeah, that sounds weird, all right. But like I said, I don't know anything about that."

"You sure, Cole? You haven't you been paging through Wikipedia? Didn't find some other articles you'd like to talk about? Did Scott have a page like Mr. Drick's? Does Winnie?"

The blue-green curtain vibrated, sure to come down at any moment. Chetley would be standing there on the other side, a tie loose around his neck, hands ready to call the cops or do something much worse.

Corduroy would never look more lethal.

But Cole was not about to find out. The door opened and the nurse strode to his side. "The doctor's here. Let's get you checked out." Cole let her trundle him off. But Chetley wasn't done.

"Do I have a Wikipedia page, Cole? Do you?"

CHAPTER 22

PainAuChoCOLEat: It was nuts.

ShesGottaGavlt: back up

ShesGottaGavlt: chetley thinks i have potential

ShesGottaGavlt: there may be hope for me yet

PainAuChoCOLEat: ARE YOU PAYING ATTENTION

PainAuChoCOLEat: CHETLEY KNOWS ABOUT THE WIKIPEDIA PAGES

ShesGottaGavlt: easy on the caps lock

PainAuChoCOLEat: ONLY WHEN I AM SATISFIED THAT YOU ARE SUFFICIENTLY CONCERNED ABOUT THE POTENTIAL FOR ARREST AND/OR DANGER

PainAuChoCOLEat: What if Josh isn't the killer?

PainAuChoCOLEat: What if it's Chetley?

ShesGottaGavlt: first you thought it was josh

ShesGottaGavlt: then you thought it was chetley

ShesGottaGavlt: then you went back to josh

ShesGottaGavlt: now you're back on chetley again

PainAuChoCOLEat: If you'd been there, you'd wonder, too. ·

ShesGottaGavlt: him eavesdropping on you is indeed cause for concern

ShesGottaGavlt: anyone else listening to you would have died of snoredom

ShesGottaGavlt: has whinny been in touch

PainAuChoCOLEat: She texted a few times while I was with the doctor.

ShesGottaGavlt: did she say anything about the wikis

PainAuChoCOLEat: Nothing.

PainAuChoCOLEat: Either she hasn't checked out her page or she thinks it's a joke.

ShesGottaGavlt: we have that going for us

ShesGottaGavlt: better that she focuses on winning you back than the prediction of her murder

PainAuChoCOLEat: I don't know for sure that she wants me back.

ShesGottaGavlt: she tried to kiss you

PainAuChoCOLEat: That could've been a momentary lapse of judgment.

PainAuChoCOLEat: Brought on by all of the trauma building up.

PainAuChoCOLEat: Maybe I don't want to get back together with her anymore.

WinWin: Hi

PainAuChoCOLEat: Maybe I want to focus on getting my grades back in shape.

PainAuChoCOLEat: And put some pep back into my baking.

PainAuChoCOLEat: Oh yeah, and keep out of jail.

ShesGottaGavlt: glad you have your priorities straight

PainAuChoCOLEat: I'm starting to wonder if I was wrong about her.

PainAuChoCOLEat: Hi.
WinWin: Phew

PainAuChoCOLEat: Say you have a girlfriend.

WinWin: I was starting to think you really were
ignoring me

ShesGottaGavlt: i like where you are going with
this so far
PainAuChoCOLEat: Say she goes berserk.
ShesGottaGavlt: with lust

PainAuChoCOLEat: Not ignoring you.
PainAuChoCOLEat: I'm just not sure what to say.
PainAuChoCOLEat: Beyond hi.

PainAuChoCOLEat: Is thought to have killed people.

WinWin: Well
WinWin: I'm the one who has things to say
PainAuChoCOLEat: Are you still pulling down
straight As?
WinWin: You don't have to do any talking at all

ShesGottaGavlt: you are holding it against her that
she still cares about her future
ShesGottaGavlt: you of all people
ShesGottaGavlt: the girl you have been pining for
wants you back

WinWin: If you'll let me
WinWin: Come over

ShesGottaGavlt: and you are going to deny her

WinWin: Everyone's out
WinWin: It'll just be you and me
PainAuChoCOLEat: Okay.
PainAuChoCOLEat: I'm going over there.
PainAuChoCOLEat: Happy?

WinWin: :)

ShesGottaGavlt: ecstatic

WinWin: See you soon

ShesGottaGavlt: was on pins and needles

<WinWin signed off>

ShesGottaGavlt: bit of advice
ShesGottaGavlt: let her work for it

WaldaWinchell: Hallo!

<ShesGottaGavlt signed off>

WaldaWinchell: How're you feeling?
PainAuChoCOLEat: Okay.

WaldaWinchell: Super.

WaldaWinchell: You'll need all your strength for the schnitzel ahead of you.

WaldaWinchell: Should I meet you there? I have a car. I can pick you up.

PainAuChoCOLEat: I can't go.

PainAuChoCOLEat: I'm really sorry.

PainAuChoCOLEat: I wouldn't bail on you if it wasn't important.

PainAuChoCOLEat: Can we do it another time?

WaldaWinchell: Are you bailing because of your ex-girlfriend who treats you like dirt?

PainAuChoCOLEat: Well, I don't have any other ex-girlfriends, but yes.

<WaldaWinchell signed off>

CHAPTER 23

Cole rode over to Winnie's after his head cleared, and now dawdled astride his bicycle out front. He waited there for several minutes, working up the nerve to ring the bell, even though she'd invited him over. She'd already taken the pressure off him, told him that she would do the talking. But he'd have to answer her at some point. He'd have to know what he'd say. And in order to know what he'd say, he'd have to know what he wanted. He'd taken the long way over, the better to figure it out. By the time he arrived at her house, he felt dumber than ever.

He knew only one thing for sure, and that was that he'd just ditched Lila to see his ex-girlfriend. Maybe Winnie was about to apologize and take him back. But then again, maybe she was already regretting almost kissing him. Maybe she was about to humiliate him some more. Maybe she'd gotten back with Josh. Maybe she was hiding him. Maybe they were about to kill him together.

The paranoia he'd picked up since Drick's death was almost as heavy a burden as the guilty conscience he was already lugging around.

Daylight fading fast, he climbed the steps to the porch and rang the doorbell.

A long moment passed as he rehearsed his opening ("Hi") and waited, clammy, for the door to open.

It didn't.

He rang again.

No one greeted him.

Maybe the long way over was too long for Winnie and she'd gotten tired of waiting for him.

The lights inside the parlor were on and cast a glow that leant the porch a faint halo. He leaned over the railing, glanced up the driveway, and spotted Winnie's Toyota parked precisely in front of the garage.

Cole returned to the front door, pressed his finger against the bell, and held it there. "Winnie? It's Cole. Sorry it took me so long. Do you still want to talk?"

No answer.

He turned to leave, muttering under his breath, "Screw this. Screw her." She sneaks into the school nurse's office, sits there next to him waiting for him to wake up, tries to kiss him, and asks him over? When no one else is home? And doesn't come to the door when he gets there? It wasn't right. It wasn't fair. He refused to stand there like a putz, hoping she'd grant him an audience. He'd go home, call Lila, humble himself, and hope the Blue Danube was still on the table, if she hadn't already taken someone else.

No, wait. Screw *that*. Not Lila. Screw walking away. Winnie didn't get to jerk him around. She owed him an explanation. She owed him an apology. She owed him the chance to judge her. And he was going to take it.

He banged on the front door and opened his mouth, ready to raise his voice, only to stop mid-breath. The door had swung open at his touch, slicing the silence inside with a creak.

"Hello?"

Cole looked back at the street, unpeopled and still, except for the big maples lining the block, their branches italicized in the wind. Winnie lived in the oldest part of Springfield, where the tree trunks are thickest and most stalwart. But they weren't so wholesome in the gloom. In this light they looked barren and jagged and crooked, the remnants of an old pier long ago washed away by the sea.

Cole stepped inside the house, wincing as the floorboards protested under his weight.

Something wasn't right.

The house was holding its breath, as though he'd walked in on it while it was up to no good. It watched him, eyes in the framed pictures and the grandfather clock, waiting to see how he would proceed before deciding whether to continue with its secret purpose.

To the left was the parlor, empty. To his right, a sitting room, dark. Beyond that, a hallway led to the back of the house. There, a powder room, a kitchen, and the dining room where Winnie's parents once hosted the debate team after winning States. There was a walk-in pantry off the kitchen, where Winnie had pulled Cole by the necktie for a celebratory make-out. Even now on some mornings he'd wake up, sure he'd just been there among the brown sugar and Honeycomb, her fingers grasping his pockets.

Before him was the staircase. At its foot, Winnie's bag. Her coat was hung over the newel post.

Cole looked up the staircase. Ten steps up was a landing. There, it hooked right and continued into shadows. He took out his phone, selected Winnie's name — still ranked at the top of his favorites, heaven help him if Gavin ever found out — and called.

A sound twisted down the stairs from some nook high in the level above. Cole couldn't immediately place the tune but knew it wasn't "Billionaire," the song Winnie had assigned his number at the height of their relationship. She'd since replaced his ringtone with something else. Probably the first thing she did after she dumped him.

Cole let the phone ring as he went up the stairs, following the sound around the landing and into the darkness. The only light at the top seeped from Winnie's room, its door ajar. He wondered if she still had the yellow comforter he'd gotten to know. He was close enough to make out the last chords of the ringtone before he was rung through to voice mail: "U Can't Touch This." He snapped his phone shut in anger.

"Winnie! It's Cole. I'm coming in."

Her room hadn't changed. The yellow comforter, the clusters of candles, the stack of *Teen Vogue*s in the corner, camouflaged with a five-year-old copy of the *New Yorker* atop them. Winnie sat at her desk, her back to him, facing her computer. It was tuned to her screen saver, a picture of herself with Josh from homecoming.

"Did you not hear me laying on the bell? Hello?"

He dared to take her arm. "Winnie, I'm talking to you!" He snatched his hand back, snakebit. The house was warm but she was cold. Cole gingerly swiveled the chair toward him. Her arm fell from the rest, her hand dangling limply above the carpet. He took a step back. Winnie wasn't Winnie anymore.

Her fingernails were broken at right angles. Her head fell to the side, unsupported, and her tongue hung out, uncorked from her open mouth, distended and blue. Cole's eyes locked onto hers, lazy slits. The white was gone, painted over with the bright, screaming red of blood burst from capillaries, ruptured by the force of strangulation. Around her neck wrapped three times tightly was the instrument of her death, her own length of hair. A dark bruise blossomed where it touched her skin.

Bile gushed up his throat. He dropped to his knees and threw up into a wastebasket. As his insides undulated he took weird note of the trash: Winnie still drank diet orange soda and chewed Orbit by the mouthful. No. Not still. Used to.

He stayed there, perched, waiting out the sick, and then longer. He couldn't bear the thought of facing Winnie again, the awful shrunkeness of her body minus breath. But he had to call for help. Eyes watering, he lifted his head, careful not to look in her direction. His gaze landed on her computer.

The screen saver had disappeared when he jostled her body. Open on the display was a Web page. Winnie's Wikipedia entry. Cole gingerly reached around her corpse and scrolled to the bottom, where Cole and Gavin had added her death, described exactly as he found her.

Below it were two lines they had not added.

Winnie Hoffman

From *Wikipedia*, the free encyclopedia

Winnie Hoffman is an **American** high school student, tennis player, and faithless girlfriend. She is best known for her academic prowess and ability to bring about the ruin of star students with the wink of an eye.[1] She might have landed valedictorian and gone on to big things and bigger boyfriends at **Harvard**, but she was undone by her vanity. Winnie Hoffman died before she could be accepted to any school, her big brain not quite big enough to figure out that her habit for betrayal might catch up to her one day, wrap itself around her neck, and squeeze the life out of her.

This article about a high school senior who broke hearts and had her own neck broken in return is a stub. *You can help Wickedpedia by* expanding *it.*

---

[1] See articles on **Josh Truffle** and **Cole Redeker**.

Cole didn't have a Wikipedia page. Not that he knew of, anyway.

His fingers hovered over the trackpad, poised to click the link. Did he want to see this? No. But he had to. Someone says *Don't think about pink elephants,* you think about pink elephants. Cole had no choice. He clicked.

Seconds later, as he surveyed the contents of the link, there came a *chuff chuff* of shoes kissing carpet and a new but familiar voice.

"Winnie?"

Josh stood in the doorway. Cole saw Winnie's body shine, reflected in Josh's crater-big eyes. His fists clenched and unclenched again and again to the silent stroke of a metronome. "You killed her!"

Cole un-hunched from over the desk. "Josh, wait."

Josh didn't.

He flung himself at Cole.

They collided. Cole popped backward, as if jerked by a string. For a split second he felt his feet leave the floor. They pedaled twice in midair as Josh drove his weight forward, their momentum propelling them both right up against Winnie's picture window.

And then through it.

And then down.

Down.

Down.

Down.

And then out.

CHAPTER 24

The first thing Cole became aware of was the sound. A beep, intermittent but steady, and fuzzy around the edges. He was warm and snuggly, swaddled in a soft blanket. Cole opened his eyes and took in his unfamiliar but recognizable surroundings. Linoleum floors, a blue-green curtain, and the high adjustable bed in which he was enthroned. Hadn't he just been here?

Cole licked his dry lips, found a glob of coagulated spittle at one corner. Also, a flap of something sticky, begging to be peeled off.

"Don't futz with your bandages, Scarface." Gavin sat in a chair at the end of the bed. "You've got more stitches on your face than blackheads. Sleep, okay?"

"Gabbin." Cole's jaw blundered one way, and his lips another. "Gabba."

"You were closer the first time," his friend said as he stepped up to Cole's side, but somehow managed to keep his distance all the same. "How are you feeling?"

"Cheerful," Cole oozed. "Like a rainbow." Yes? Yes. Surely rainbows spent their days feeling as bubbly as he did now.

"Wow," Gavin said, tapping an IV channeled into Cole's arm. "They gave you the good stuff. If there's any left by the time you're sprung, smuggle it out with you."

"Gavin." Cole hit the *V* with an effort. Articulating every syllable demanded parallel parking–level concentration, and to Cole's knowledge, rainbows didn't drive.

"Yes, dear?"

"Am I dead?"

A second passed as Gavin beheld him, expressionless, and then another, a pause loaded like the moment after you confessed to a girl you like-liked her, and before she made your life or made you lifeless. Finally Gavin smiled. Something about it felt weird to Cole, but then, the rainbow sensation was foreign to him, too. "No, dude. You've been knocked out since the ambulance picked you up this afternoon. You got banged up stuntman-style, and thanks to the broken glass you look like your face lost a fight with a sack of supremely pissed off woodpeckers. But no. You're not dead. Your parents are outside, chatting it up with your doctors. If my eavesdropping skills are up to snuff, you'll be out of the hospital in a few days."

Cole squinted, thinking. The room listed to one side and back. He closed his eyes and opened them. "Did I fall?"

"Right through a window, with Josh clinging to you like you were caught up in some operatic gay suicide pact. Is there something you've been keeping from me, Cole?"

"I fell," Cole said. Fragments of memories were smushed together in his head with all the clarity of an elementary-school-art-class collage. Winnie's house. Winnie's hair. Winnie's computer. Winnie's boyfriend. His thoughts clicked. "Josh pushed me. He pushed me and we went out the window!" It sounded like a sitcom punch line, minus the laugh track. "Because of Winnie."

"Yeah," Gavin said, his voice softening. "Because of Winnie. You saw what happened to her?"

"She's dead, Gavin." His face was suddenly wet. A salty tear tipped over his upper lip and into his mouth. "He killed her. Josh killed her."

Gavin looked away. Embarrassed at Cole's display or emotional because of it, Cole couldn't tell. "I know, buddy. I'm sorry" was all he could say.

Cole sat straight up. "We have to stop him."

"It's okay, Cole."

"You don't understand. He killed Winnie. He must've killed Drick and Scott, too. We have to stop him."

"Don't worry about Josh. He's not going to kill anyone else."

"But he could! We have to find him!"

"No we don't," Gavin said. "I can tell you where he is right now. Two floors down in the ICU."

"You're not making any sense. I see you, too."

"The Intensive Care Unit. Trust me. Chances are Josh won't kill anyone else ever again. His spine shattered when you two hit the ground."

Cole heard the words. They were definitely English. But he couldn't make heads or tails of them. "But you said I'm going to be fine."

Gavin put on his "patient" voice, which was less "patient" than it was "superior." "Yeah, because he went splat underneath you and you went all bouncy castle right off his muscle and meat. Guess all that soccer was good for something, huh? He saved your bacon."

"But he's going to be okay, right?"

"I guess. As long as the guys in cellblock D don't use him as a go-kart. Josh's gonna be rolling for the rest of his life."

There was a kid at school, Adam somebody, who used a wheelchair. They didn't share any classes but Cole knew from Gavin's complaining that he got let out a few minutes early every period to head off to his next class, a luxury Gavin sorely desired because "Add up all those minutes and it amounts to an extra nap every week, two if you like 'em short." Cole felt as though every time he saw Adam it was at the opposite end of a hallway, and he was just turning a corner, wheeling out of sight. He wondered what it would be like to live life as a mirage, to be seen and not seen at the same time.

Gavin saw Cole's conscience wrestling Josh's injury on his face. "Don't feel bad about it. So what if he never walks again, never kicks another ball? He got what he deserved. If it wasn't clear before, it is now. He killed people. And not just any people. He killed Winnie." Cole put his hands over his eyes. Hearing Gavin say it was different than saying it himself. Cole's chest began to jerk and spasm. Gavin pretended not to notice. "But now he's screwed, and you're the one who screwed him. You're a hero."

Cole looked up at Gavin, his eyes red. "I am?" he snarled.

"It's all over the news! Spring Showers has been camped out in the parking lot ever since you got here, competing with a slew of other reporters to bag you for an exclusive. You'll be glad to know I selflessly allowed her to bag me instead. For an interview, that is."

"No," Cole burbled. "I can't. I can't see reporters." His head was oppressed by the image of Winnie, dead at her desk, slumped over like she'd been deboned. "They'll ask me things. I can't talk about it. I can't even think about it."

"You don't have to talk to the reporters if you don't want to." Now Gavin's voice was mild, a chain-restaurant salsa. "But you are gonna have to talk to the police. Not right now. But soon. When you're done and over your rainbow. They're gonna want to hear what happened straight from your mouth. So they can put this whole thing to rest. You can swing that, right? For Winnie?"

Cole doubted he could. But he knew he had to.

Gavin looked behind him, then back at Cole. His voice was lower now. "And when you do talk to them, do us both a favor and remember what we talked about last time, okay? Leave out the whole Wikipedia revenge-plot aspect. No sense confusing the 'Valedictorian Catches Serial Killer' narrative with behavior some might call bush-league, right?"

"But I'm not valedictorian!"

Gavin cocked his head. "I think we both know you will be now. Congratulations in advance." He got up to go. "Time to get ready for my close-up. Spring is expecting an update."

"Gavin?"

"Yes, dear?"

"Are you sure I'm not dead?"

"Sure I'm sure. If you were dead, I'd be dead. And I'm kicking. So, so are you." He walked out before he could hear Cole add something out loud, for his own ears.

"For now."

Gavin hadn't seen what happened in Winnie's room, nor what was on her computer when Cole clicked the link for his name. Soupy as his thoughts were, he managed to piece together what he'd read on the screen.

Cole Redeker

From *Wikipedia*, the free encyclopedia

Cole Redeker is an **American** high school student of little significance. He thought he was smart. He thought he was talented. He thought he was entitled to a bright future. He was wrong. He died stewing in his own juices.

There on the screen was Cole's life. And the date of his death.
December 12.
One week from his fall.
This weekend.

CHAPTER 25

When his doctors agreed to let Cole go home, it was days later — the date fixed for his expiration. His stay in the hospital was marked by an endless march of Mylar balloons and stuffed animals gifted from newly admiring SHS females who'd never, not once, even sneered his way; Spring Showers, intrepid inept reporter was twice caught sneaking into his room, once in scrubs and a face mask and again posing as the hospital librarian; the mayor's announcement that the street leading to the school would be renamed "Redeker Road"; and Winnie's burial.

Cole would not attend.

His parents and doctors refused to consider discharging him in time for the service. "You sustained two head injuries in one day," said his neurologist, waving Cole's brain scan, a mosaic of inkblots.

He was secretly grateful for their veto. It was a scuzzy feeling, but surely it was better than purging his grief and guilt all over a church full of Winnie's friends and family. Reading her obituary was all it took to rumble up great, bone-seizing sobs. Cole was certain if he didn't spontaneously combust just setting foot inside the church, he'd disintegrate as soon he saw her casket. By his logic, he was right to stay away. That became obvious when the police finally came for him.

"I know you're going through a hard time right now so we'll take this nice and easy," Detective Simms told Cole, though he got the feeling it was said for the benefit of his parents and the lawyer they'd hired to represent his interests, all of them crammed into his hospital room. On the other side of the curtain came the hollering snore of his roommate, Mrs. Osborn, a septuagenarian with operable sleep apnea. Cole was glad to know his misery wasn't keeping her up. "I just need to hear your account of what happened," Simms said.

"What happened to the other detective?" Cole asked.

"What other detective?"

"I never got his name," Cole said. "The one who talked to me at school . . . after my teacher got killed."

"You mean Morris," said Simms. "He needed a break, and we decided to go in another direction with this investigation."

Cole wondered whether a new detective wearing a coffee-stained tie was really the new direction the police should be taking. "Don't you already know what happened?" he asked. "Gavin said it was all over the news days ago."

"I'm sorry, Gavin?" Simms asked, stooped over Cole with a notepad and pen in hand, his bald spot glaring like a spotlight. "Who's Gavin?"

The question was not asked of her, but Cole's mother was raring to answer it anyway. "Just the neighborhood hoodlum."

"And my best friend," said Cole. "We were together at school when we found Drick, Mr. Drick, I mean," he corrected.

"And he told you what?"

"That the story had already hit the news. Why, what's wrong with that?"

"Nothing." Scribble. "Just getting my facts straight. Tell me about the night you went over to Winnie's."

"What do you want to know?"

"Why were you there?"

"She invited me to come."

"Did that seem strange to you?"

"Why would it? We were friends. Sort of."

"Sort of friends?"

"We weren't very close before she . . ." Cole swallowed and held his breath, then began again. "Before Josh killed her."

Simms persisted. "But you were closer at one time before?"

"She was my girlfriend. But we weren't so close anymore because she broke up with me to go out with someone else."

"And that someone else would be Josh Truffle?"

"Yes. Him."

"And you and Josh used to be friends, is that right?"

"Who told you that? Josh?"

"Was I told wrong?" Simms breezed, as if they were all friends here.

"We played soccer together when we were kids. We never got much closer than that."

"Sounds like you don't like him."

"What's to like?"

"Easy, Cole," warned his father.

"No, Dad. I used to feel bad about Josh's troubles and I suppose I should feel even worse now that he can't walk. But now I can see him for what he really is and I won't pretend otherwise."

"What is he?" asked Simms.

"An entitled jerk. The administration cushioned his grades to keep him from getting kicked off the soccer team. He made an art of cheating and plagiarizing, making fools of everyone else who followed the rules, and the minute he got caught he acted like he deserved to get a special dispensation from the consequences! He bullied Winnie into staying with him when she knew better, but when she finally got her back up and cut him loose, he killed her for it! After he'd probably already killed his best friend and my teacher!"

"Probably? You don't sound so sure."

In fact, part of Cole wasn't so sure. Hadn't Josh accused him of killing Winnie when he came into her room?

"What does it matter whether or not I'm sure?! I'm not a detective!"

"Cole," his mother said, trying to interrupt with all the oomph of a cobweb.

"But instead of detecting how Josh came to choke Winnie to death, you'd rather take me on a walk down memory lane to when we were eight years old and he stole my Gatorade at soccer camp!"

Cole's lawyer sniffed and called a halt to the interview. "My client is distraught."

"Just a few more questions, counselor? You can do a few more questions, right, Cole? When you entered the house, did you notice anything out of the ordinary? Anything out of place?"

"No. But I hadn't been inside since before we'd broken up. How would I know if something was weird?"

"Go on. You went up the stairs."

"The light in her room was on. I went in. She was at her desk. Something was wrong. Her hair. It was around her neck."

Squeezing.

Constricting.

Drowning her insides with dead air.

Was she waiting for him? Did she think he'd come for her?

Did she know who killed her?

Did she think it was him?

Did she die thinking he'd murdered her?

"She was strangled with her own hair. She was dead."

Cole heard a sound like the opening of a can of soda and looked toward it. His father's arm was around his mother. They were shedding tears, their faces contorted. Their breathing labored. If Cole hadn't already seen Winnie's body, his parents' woe would have been the worst thing ever.

Simms cleared his throat and looked up from his notes. "When did Josh arrive?"

"After I —"

He stopped.

"After you what?"

After Cole saw Winnie's death chronicled and his own death foretold on Wikipedia pages.

After he saw the Wikipedia pages that could incriminate him.

Gavin was right. Telling the truth might only make it harder to punish Josh.

And Josh needed to be punished.

"He showed up after I vomited." It was the truth. Some of it, at least. "I saw Winnie and got sick. Then Josh came. He said, 'You killed her.' Then he came at me and we went through the window. The next thing I knew I was here. I don't know what happened in between."

"It was just a few minutes before the ambulance and uniforms arrived," said Simms. "A Good Samaritan saw you fall and called 9-1-1 right away."

"We'd like to thank that person," Cole's mother said.

"So would I," said Simms. "But whoever it was didn't stick around, and the phone company says the call was made from a burner." Cole's parents didn't know what that meant. "A pre-paid, disposable cell phone. No name attached to it."

Cole's lawyer cleared his throat. Cole had forgotten he was there and wondered if he'd dozed off. "Is that all, detective?"

Cole needed it to be all, before his chest caved in and sucked him into himself, leaving just his hospital ID bracelet. Simms drew a finger across his lip.

"Last thing, I promise. Why do you think Josh said what he did? Why do you think he told you that you killed her?"

The detective was thinking the same thing Cole was. "Maybe he blamed me for making him kill her. Maybe he's crazy. I don't know why he said it. All I know is he killed her."

"How do you know? You didn't actually see him do it."

"Because I just do. I told you, the front door was open when I got there. Someone had already gone inside and killed her. It was Josh."

"The front door was open, sure," Simms said. "But the back door was locked. Did you know that, Cole?"

Simms was getting at something. Cole didn't know what it was, but he knew it wasn't good.

"See, Winnie knew we were looking for Josh. She knew we strongly suspected him of killing his friend and his teacher. Winnie's parents knew this, too. They told me they were very careful to lock the doors after they left for work the day she died. Her father called her from work after she got home from school to make sure she'd locked the front door again behind her. She told him she had. So it leaves me with a problem. Why was the back door locked, but not the front door?"

Cole yearned for a mute button. "I don't know."

"Here's one theory on how that came to be," Simms said. "Winnie got home from school, let herself in, and locked the door behind her. A while later someone rings the doorbell. She looks out the window and sees that her caller is someone she knows. Someone she doesn't believe is dangerous. Someone she trusts. Maybe even someone she's expecting. So she unlocks the door and lets them in."

If Cole's mother had been wearing pearls, she would have clutched them. "Just what are you trying to say, Detective Simms?"

Simms licked his lips.

"I'm just saying it's interesting."

He'd shucked the look of the shambling, nice-and-easy detective just out to fill in some blanks, and revealed a more authentic expression. He leered at Cole, all teeth. Cole knew this look. He saw it every time someone caught the aroma of his latest confectionary experiment. The detective was famished. And Cole was his meal.

"What he's trying to say, Mrs. Redeker," came Mrs. Osborn's squeak from beyond the curtain, "is that Josh isn't his only suspect." Her snoring had stopped long ago, just as Cole's troubles were taking a turn for the worse.

CHAPTER 26

Cole was released the next day. Per hospital policy, he climbed into a wheelchair and allowed a nurse to trundle him down to the lobby, where his mother waited. His father looped around the hospital grounds in the car until they were ready to make a run for it, weaving through the gauntlet of reporters gathered outside hoping for a quote from Springfield's hero, "Winnie's Avenger." What they didn't know — what no one knew, thanks to the tight lid the police were keeping on the investigation — was that the police regarded him as a potential killer, right along with Josh. But during the course of the interview, Detective Simms had hardly mentioned Drick or Scott. Did the police think Josh killed them both? Had they still not picked up on the Wikipedia pages? Or were they waiting to spring more accusations on Cole during another surprise interrogation? Whom were they after? Why hadn't Josh just confessed and finally put an end to this?

"Here he comes," Cole's mother said, spotting his father's Camry darting up the driveway to the hospital entrance.

Cole got up and went back the way he came. "Tell him to make another pass, Mom. I forgot something upstairs."

"Cole, I want to get out of here."

"Me too. Couple of minutes, that's all."

The elevator doors closed behind him, cutting off her clucking. He had a feeling he'd need more than a few minutes. But he had a visit to make, and he couldn't leave the hospital until it was concluded.

Admittance to the ICU was controlled by nurses stationed opposite clear Plexiglas doors that locked and unlocked at their discretion. Cole didn't know if visitors were limited to close family, but he wouldn't take any chances. When the nurse on duty looked up and released the locks, he had his story ready.

"I'm here to see my grandmother."

"Name?"

"Uh, Osborn." The splintery old lady had suffered complications during her operation. "Gramma Osborn." Cole had never asked her for her first name, and if she'd volunteered it, he'd tuned her out.

"I can see the resemblance," the nurse warbled. "Delia's a sweetheart. You're a good boy to come visit her." The nurse pointed to a corridor leading away from reception. "Down the hall, take a left. First room on the right. And don't forget to sanitize those hands."

Cole prowled by stores of supplies, drawers of bandages and syringes, unattached IVs, and empty gurneys idling outside dimly lit rooms. Inside those rooms, patients seesawed between life and death. Tiny sounds crept into the corridor, the whooshes and blips of ventilators and cardiac monitors keeping time to the coo of a loved one's prayers. Cole ducked a glance into each room, on the hunt.

A police officer dozed on a stool by a door at the end of the hall, his hand loose around an empty coffee cup. Cole knew the patient inside wasn't going anywhere. Not in his condition. There was only one reason the cop had any business sitting there.

He was there to protect the patient from someone who might do him harm.

Someone like Cole.

The cop's head bowed and jerked twice, as if in response to some dreamed question. Cole retreated into a pantry and put on a fresh pot of coffee. The scent of roasted Arabica slithered down the hall and curled around the cop. He awoke, took a quick look back inside the room, and went off in search of caffeine. Cole let himself into the room the cop had left behind, closed the door behind him, and drew the blinds.

A lamp on a side table cast a warm glow over the room. Whirring, hissing machines kept solemn council around a bed. In it lay Josh. Purple bruises rampaged across his skin, where it wasn't already wrapped in gauze or casts. A skullcap of white bandages was fitted to his head, immobilized by a neck brace. Cole could not look directly at his face, which was less a face than a collection of human features cut into puzzle pieces, mixed with other puzzles, never to properly fit again. Josh was nearly turned inside out, his nose a crater, his eyes so swollen shut they looked swallowed whole. An erector set of metal rods kept order over his broken bones.

Cole squeezed his fists. He had come seeking answers. A confession. He wanted Josh to tell him he'd killed Winnie and Scott and Drick. He wanted to know why.

He wanted to know none of it was his fault.

And if he couldn't get any of that, he wanted Josh to hurt. Cole wanted to break his spirit. But looking at him now, Cole knew that wasn't possible. There was nothing left to break in Josh that wasn't already broken. Cole turned to go.

"Water?" The word rasped from Josh's mouth.

Josh was still, his eyes closed. But he was awake. He sensed a presence. But he didn't sense it was Cole's.

"Thirsty."

A bowl of water sat on the side table. A small sponge floated inside it.

"Please?"

Cole wanted to walk out. Let Josh suffer. Let his lips chap and run red. Let his throat scorch and burn. He'd done worse to Winnie.

Instead Cole picked up the sponge and dabbed it against Josh's mouth. The clear liquid trickled inside, and down his face. He blotted and swallowed.

"Thank you."

Cole put the sponge down and stepped back.

"You don't have to go. You could stay."

Cole looked at the mush before him, trying to fish out the features of the kid he'd once called his friend, before girls and grades, growing up and growing jealousy had drifted between them.

"Don't wanna be alone."

Next to the bed was a chair. On it rested an issue of *Teen Vogue*. Its cover featured Taylor Swift in a top hat. Cole set it aside, sat down, and waited.

"It's okay. You don't have to say anything," Josh said. "Nobody knows what to say to me," Josh said. "Doesn't stop them from trying, though."

The longer Cole looked at Josh, the less like a root vegetable he appeared. There was something human there. Maybe not very human. But just human enough.

"I keep thinking about Winnie." He stopped and gulped. "It was sick. Her hair tied around her neck. And Cole standing there. That freak. I didn't even think. I screamed and ran at him and we went through the window. Now here I am. And she's gone." He hocked back snot. "I'm lucky to be alive. That's what people say when they can't think of anything else. So stupid. I wasn't lucky to see my girlfriend disfigured. I'll never forget it no matter how hard I try. It's not fair. If she had to die, I should have died, too. And Cole. Cole most of all." A new fact pinballed through Cole's head, breaking down everything that he'd wanted so desperately to believe.

When Josh found Cole in Winnie's room, he'd expected to find her alive.

Josh hadn't killed her.

Cole pushed to his feet, his head gorged with new questions.

"Where are you going?" asked Josh.

Out. Away. Anywhere but here.

"I didn't mean to upset you. Don't go."

Cole turned to escape but stumbled into the chair, knocking the magazine off the side table. It flapped to the floor. He picked it up, the habit of a neatnik.

"Stay a little while longer, okay?" Josh begged plaintively, a little boy whose father had to leave for work. "You didn't even tell me the results of my quiz."

A voice in the corridor.

Cole risked a peek outside. The police officer had returned with his cup of coffee, but was busy blocking another would-be visitor.

"Sorry, miss. If you're not on the list, you don't see Josh."

"I just want a minute to ask him a few questions, officer." The cop's heft blocked Cole's vision of the girl, but he knew her by her rhythm. "It's for a story I'm writing. I'm a member of the press!" Lila fussed, trying to squirt by the cop. "The public has a right to know!" Cole felt Josh stir behind him.

"Who is that out there?"

Cole slipped out and took off in the opposite direction from Lila and the cop, but not before she spotted him. "Why is it okay for the guy who almost died with Josh to see him but I can't?"

The cop whirled. But Cole was already speeding around the corner, all the way through the ward until he'd arrived back at the nurses' station. "Did you and Delia have a good visit?" asked the nurse. Cole was out the door without answering, zipping into a stairwell as he heard Lila skid up to the reception area, too far behind to catch up now. He took the stairs two at a time, running from Josh, from Lila, from the cop, from a question he couldn't shake.

If Josh hadn't killed Winnie, who had?

Cole's mother was still waiting in the lobby. Together they piled into the car and his father drove off. His mother turned around from the front seat and glared. "Is that what you had to run upstairs for, keeping us waiting?"

Cole looked in his hand. He didn't remember rolling up the magazine in Josh's room and taking it with him. He relaxed his grip and *Teen Vogue* splayed out on his lap.

His mother wrinkled her nose. "Since when do you read that?"

"I don't," Cole breathed, his eyes fixed on the name of the addressee listed on the mailing label. But he now knew someone who did.

Andrea Henderson.

CHAPTER 27

Cole first noticed the green ribbons when his father turned into their subdivision. He'd been too busy looking behind the trees for potential assassins, not at them. One green ribbon was tied in a bow around each tree trunk. "What's with those?" Cole wondered if they were meant to honor a fallen soldier, but thought the appropriate color was yellow, or maybe black, not green.

His mother looked at his father, then out the window. They knew this was coming, but knowing didn't make telling him any easier. "They're for Winnie."

Tree after tree was dressed for her death.

Would they be dressed for his come tomorrow morning? After all, it was the day Winnie's killer had marked for Cole's murder. He took shallow breaths, afraid he might hyperventilate right there in the car.

"Why green?" Cole asked.

"It's the color for missing children. It's the closest they could get."

Apparently the mourning industry had not yet assigned a color to "Murdered by Ex-Boyfriend."

A host of neighbors and students was assembled outside his front door. They carried signs congratulating his recovery. They cheered as Cole's father pulled up the driveway. "Welcome home."

It would have been a fine sentiment had Cole been worthy

of it. But he had done nothing to prevent Winnie's death, and maybe only hastened it. And the more he pondered, the surer he was that her killer was still on the loose. The canyon of heroes was treatment misplaced, and he could have done without his mother snapping photos to augment his college applications and the microphone meal Spring Showers forced on him when he stepped out of the car. "How does it feel to have caught Winnie's murderer? If you could say anything to Josh right now, what would it be?"

Gavin dislodged himself from the crowd and nudged Spring to the side. "Given our hero's knack for culinary arts I think he'd go with something along the lines of, 'Let justice be served.'" The crowd applauded Gavin's oration as he helped hustle Cole inside.

The turnout dissipated as soon as the door closed behind him. Spring and her crew hung on for a few more hours, recording interviews with neighbors and passersby, every once in a while aiming a camera at the house, hoping to nab a glimpse of movement or a wave. Cole wished they'd just go away. "Want me to moon them?" Gavin asked. "Never mind, that'd have the opposite effect." Finally Spring packed it in and took off, the light waning and Gavin's patience along with it.

"Of course the cops are going to wonder if you had a hand in Winnie's death," he droned after Cole told him about the interview and his encounter with Josh. "They'd be pretty bad at their job if they didn't. You were on the scene. You discovered her body. She'd broken up with you. But they have a couple more reasons to believe Josh was to blame, and their names are Scott and Drick."

"It's not just the cops," Cole fretted. "It's my Wikipedia page. Do you know I'm supposed to die today?"

"Hey, me too," said Gavin. "Brothers until the end."

Cole could've kicked himself.

"It never occurred to you that someone would ever care about me enough to want me dead, did it." Gavin hadn't phrased it like a question.

"I'm sorry. I didn't mean to get so wrapped up in myself. I didn't think."

"Yeah, you forget to do that every now and then," Gavin chuckled. "Don't worry about it. You were always tops on Josh's hit list. Me, I was low-hanging fruit. He'd have gotten around to me eventually, whenever he decided he could be bothered. But in the meantime, I promise, I'd have raised many a glass to my dearly departed best friend."

"You may still have that opportunity," warned Cole. "I think we're wrong about Josh. I don't think he killed anyone."

Cole told Gavin the story of his visit to Josh's bedside.

Gavin couldn't believe they were back to this. "And you base this theory on what, your infallible intuition? The mind-meld you formed when you and Josh dove out Winnie's window? A couple days ago you were convinced he was a psycho killer. A couple of head injuries and a single one-sided conversation later and you've come to Jesus?"

"You didn't hear him," Cole said, his voice flat.

But Gavin didn't need to. "If he didn't do it, who did? Who wanted all three of them dead? Can you think of a single person?"

Cole could not. "But just because I can't think of someone

doesn't mean there's no one who fits the bill. I'm not Sherlock Holmes."

"That's the first sensible thing you've said since 'Let's eat,' and that was weeks ago. Let it go. It's over. We could be having fun tonight, trying to get back to normal. The drama kids are throwing a huge party since the winter formal got canceled. You should come with me."

A bomb detonated in Cole. "Winnie's dead! Josh can't walk! There's a killer on the loose and you want to go to some party?! What's wrong with you?! Do you have a human bone in your body?!"

Gavin went scarlet. "We played a prank, Cole. A prank of your own design. It got out of control. But we did not kill anyone. Josh made that happen. I know you're weeping for Winnie on the inside, and I'm sorry about that." Nothing about Gavin's demeanor backed that up. "But it wasn't your fault she chose a crazy boyfriend. It was hers."

Cole flared. "It wouldn't be so easy for you to blame the victim if you'd ever —"

"What?"

"Nothing."

"Come on. Let's hear it. 'If I ever,' what? Got a girlfriend of my own?"

Yes. "If you ever cared about someone." Better.

Gavin rolled his eyes. "Yeah. Look at all the death and destruction I'm missing out on, being so antisocial and unremarkable. 'Gee, I could have a real future as a simpering imbecile . . . if only I got a girlfriend!' If the alternative to turning into a mess like you is never going steady, sign me up for the single life." He picked up his jacket. "And a friendless one. I don't need this. I don't need you."

Gavin left, maybe taking their friendship with him. Cole tried to put his advice to work. He tried to let it all go. But the police car parked down the street made that impossible. They were watching him. And waiting. Distracted, looking at the wrong person while someone else got away with three murders. Cole was no Sherlock, but he knew more than the police did. And that put it on him to figure out who was killing people and using the Wikipedia pages he'd written as cover. As if avenging Winnie and halting the ticking clock hanging over his head wasn't already reason enough.

Cole pushed the stack of assignments and college applications off his desk onto the floor, and fired up his computer. His e-mail was chock-full of messages. The latest was a reminder of the underground party going on tonight. It was being held in the empty restaurant space next to Benito's. Cole deleted the e-mail and quickly scanned the rest, finding nothing of note. He opened his browser and called up all the Wikipedia pages he and Gavin had made in a happier time, when a little revenge mischief wasn't liable to get someone killed.

Scott's. Andrea's. Drick's. Winnie's. Josh's.

He scoured them for something new. Something different. Something he may have missed every other time he pored over them. He found nothing. All of them showed a history of creation and editing using Cole's handle. Scott's and Drick's were still exactly as he and Gavin had written them, and their Wiki deaths were metaphors for their real ones. The only change to Winnie's was the added stub Cole had first noticed when he found her. Andrea's and Josh's were more or less on target, except for the fact that she'd survived and no one had actually tried to kill him.

Then there was the entry Cole hadn't written. The entry the killer had written for him. Cole wondered how his death would come to pass, if the killer got their way. He remembered the entry had concluded with something about him stewing in his own juices. Something cooking-related. He shivered. Whoever was imagining his termination had some boiling in mind. He typed his name into Wikipedia and hit SEARCH.

> Did you mean: **_école_** redeker
> The page "Cole redeker" does not exist. You can ask for it to be created, but consider checking the search results below to see whether the topic is already covered.
> For search help, please visit Help:Searching.

Cole rubbed his forehead, retyped his name and once more hit SEARCH, only to get the same results.

His page was gone. Like it had never existed.

Had he dreamed it? No. His memory of everything up until the moment he and Josh went out the window was sharp. Winnie's computer had been on. Her Wikipedia page was on the monitor. He'd clicked on a link to his name, and that had brought up his page. Cole toggled to Winnie's page. There at the bottom of the page was the footnote.

[1]See articles on **Josh Truffle** and **Cole Redeker**.

He clicked his name and his browser immediately returned with a meadow vista as seen through a cracked window.

The link was broken; his page was gone. Taken down and erased.

Cole grabbed the bag he'd taken home with him from the hospital and pulled out a folder. Detective Simms had given him copies of crime scene photos taken in Winnie's bedroom (minus her body). "When you have a chance, give them a look," Simms had said. Cole sorted through the photos and quickly found what he was looking for.

Then he called the police station and asked for Simms.

"You told me to look at the crime scene photos and tell you if anything strikes me. Well something strikes me."

"Yeah?" asked Simms wearily. "What's that?"

"Winnie's computer is off. When Josh found me and we fought, it was on."

"You're sure?"

"I'm positive," Cole said. "The browser was open."

"Open to what?"

"You don't know?" Cole's heart thumped.

"We've had trouble with the computer," said Simms. "IT is on it, but it seems as though it was tampered with. I'm not sure we'll ever know what was on it, or at least not anytime soon. What was the browser open to, Cole?"

Cole thought hard in the two seconds he gave himself to answer. Be specific with Simms now and the patrol car at the end of the street might be picking him up and delivering him to lockup in minutes. "Wikipedia," Cole blurted before he knew what he was doing.

"Which page?"

"The main page." That would have to suffice. "I guess she was doing some research. Sorry to bother you." He hung up.

Three important facts slid into place.

1. Someone had come into Winnie's room between the time he and Josh hit the ground and the police arrived.

2. That person had the expertise to obliterate the evidence on Winnie's computer that a prediction of her own death was featured on her screen, as well as the browser history that would show Cole had clicked on his own. Whoever it was had taken a big risk to keep those pages from hitting the wider public.

3. That person had gotten in and gotten out very fast. Simms told him during the questioning that the police and EMTs had arrived at Winnie's house mere minutes after the fall.

That someone — Cole was sure it was the killer — had to have been nearby, watching, keeping an eye on the house maybe from the moment Cole arrived, and then Josh. That person knew exactly how much time was needed to get the job done.

Chetley could have done it.

He knew computers. He was creepy. And he'd overheard Cole's conversation with Winnie. He knew she wanted to see him.

But Cole kept coming back to why? Why would Chetley want all those people dead? And why pin it all on Cole? Because he was a garden-variety psycho?

It was too easy, like a trick SAT question. The obvious answer was not the answer.

So what if Chetley figured out Cole might be stopping by Winnie's that night? She could have told anyone what her plans were.

Then Cole remembered something else.

She had.

Josh told Cole himself when he thought he was talking to Andrea. The memory played out in his head like a re-run. *I keep thinking about Winnie,* Josh had said. *We were going to work it out. The way she said we would. I went to see her like you told me to and she just . . .*

Andrea had been in touch with Josh that day. She advised him to take another shot with Winnie, to look for her that night, exactly when Cole would be there.

Cole's shoulders were hitched high to his ears. His pulse shot up and down with the force of a piston. He was getting closer. But he needed more.

Cole called up Twitter. He couldn't remember the nonsensical handle of the follower he sought, but he knew where to find it. He found Andrea's name and called up her Tweet history.

There it was, peppering her timeline.

Rabid Doc Lenten @ABrindleDocent

ABrindleDocent was an anagram for *Rabid Doc Lenten*. Neither of these phrases made a lick of sense to Cole. But maybe there was a third anagram that did. He reached into the recesses of his closet and unearthed an old copy of Scrabble. Blood quickening in his veins, he dumped out letters reading *a-b-r-i-n-d-l-e-d-o-c-e-n-t* and began rearranging them to see if they'd fit his suspicion.

The letters came together right away and Cole sat back on his haunches, sapped. ABRINDLEDOCENT = Rabid Doc Lenten = Benedict Arnold. Benedict Arnold = subject of a paper written by someone in Drick's class.

Gavin.

Benedict Arnold = traitor

Traitor = Gavin

His best friend.

He felt as if he'd entered a highway doing eighty on an exit ramp. The truth was hurtling toward him head-on, just out of reach —

— in *Teen Vogue.*

The magazine that Andrea had discarded in Josh's ICU lay at Cole's feet. He picked it up. Sick to his stomach, afraid of what he might find, he flipped to the 1D love-match quiz. The quiz had been taken in pen. Answers were checked off. A tally scored. A match made. A boy-band boy circled.

Cole put the magazine down and held his head while everything went not-so-funhouse topsy-turvy. Everything was circumstantial. But it all fit. He only needed a single piece of hard evidence to prove his theory right.

He also needed to know why.

A while later, when he was sure he would not ralph, when he'd devised a plan of attack, when he was sure he could speak without screaming, he picked up his phone and selected a name from his contacts.

As the call connected, he made a mental checklist of the things that he'd have to do to pull this off. One of them he crossed off.

~~Call the cops~~

As sure as Cole was, there was still a chance he was wrong. A chance that the guilt and paranoia he'd nurtured for weeks had swelled beyond his control, like an exotic pet overgrown and mauling its master. If he involved the police and was wrong, he'd have ruined lives needlessly and made himself look even guiltier. If he involved the police too soon, his target might eel out of punishment. And if he left the police out of it altogether and was right, he could wind up dead.

Cole made a decision. He had started this. And he would end it. Alone.

Well, mostly alone.

"Hello?"

"Hey," Cole said. "It's me."

"I gathered that from the caller ID," Gavin replied.

Cole didn't beat around the bush. "I'm sorry about the things I said."

Silence on the other end.

"I was a jerk. I haven't been thinking straight. You stuck by me through everything and you deserve better than a friend like me."

Further silence. This was not surprising. Gavin was unaccustomed to receiving apologies. Giving them was another matter.

"Apology accepted, I guess," came his voice. "Is that what people say?"

"When they mean it."

"Then I did it right. Sorry if I hurt your feelings," Gavin said.

"Thanks. I was thinking about what you said."

"Which part?"

"The getting back to normal part. I have to put everything behind me."

Gavin agreed. "So what do you want to do about it?"

"Are you still going to that party?"

They made their plans to meet and Cole hung up. He had one more call to make. Lila answered on the first ring.

"*Hallo*, Cole. No longer avoiding me?"

"What are you doing tonight?"

"Writing a story that implicates you in the murders of Scott, Winnie, and Drick. And you?"

"Taking you on a date."

Cole could hear her sit up straight. "Excuse me? A date?"

"You can turn it into a story. Think of it as a human-interest piece. 'My date with a killer.' Even though we both know I didn't kill anyone."

"We do?"

"Meet me at the party tonight. You know the one. In the empty restaurant next to Benito's. And do yourself a favor: Bring your digital recorder. You'll want to get extensive quotes."

Cole ended the call and quieted his vibrating insides. He felt calmer than he had in months. But he knew that wouldn't last. In a couple of hours, one of three things would happen:

1. He'd be proven totally wrong and lose everything in the process.
2. He'd catch Winnie's killer.
3. Winnie's killer would catch and kill him — on the very day Wikipedia had foreseen it.

Cole couldn't dwell on it anymore. His plan was in place. He'd see it through and hope for the best.

And in the meantime, he had baking to do.

CHAPTER 28

Springfield Police Officer Larry Breslin checked his watch and flapped a sigh over his lips. Eleven p.m. Not even midnight yet. Just one hour into this godforsaken shift. Seven more to go. He did not know what he had done to rate this deathly dull assignment. The sergeant called it "suspect safekeeping." Breslin knew that was just a fancy name for being reduced to glorified guard duty.

And what was he guarding the kid from? True, it was possible the family or friends of one of Truffle's alleged murder victims might drop by to exact retribution, but what would be the point? Breslin looked in on the patient, asleep in his bed, scaffolded with casts, IVs, and wrappings. There was hardly anything left of the kid after his fall. He was Jell-O setting in a mold. Tip him too far any one way and he was likely to pour out.

Breslin wanted out. Night shift in the ICU was the worst. All these people with one foot in the grave. Gave him the shakes.

Nurse Janikowski was the ICU's saving grace. She moseyed down the corridor carrying a cup of coffee from the pantry. It tasted like a puddle of diesel left to warm in the sun, but it kept him awake. And the company was friendly. Truffle was under orders from his lawyer not to talk to his minder, so the coffee visits amounted to the only human interaction Breslin got these nights — unless you counted Truffle's night terrors. They descended on Josh every evening, a few hours after he nodded off. His slumber would swing from silent to full-on squall in an instant. His limbs would jerk and flop. *If his arms and legs weren't already broken,* Breslin thought, *he'd wind up breaking them again with all that thrashing.* Janikowski had called on Breslin once or twice to help quell Truffle's attacks. It was the only time he felt useful on his shift, even if it scared the bejeezus out of him, because the kid never remembered it the next day. Whatever was going on in the kid's head, it was so bad he had to bury it.

Janikowski handed Breslin his coffee. "My gift to you." She said it every time. "How's the patient? Any sign he'll treat us to one of his screaming fits tonight?"

"None yet." Breslin sipped. "But it's still early." He sipped again. "Relatively early."

"As if that kid doesn't have enough problems to contend with," she lamented. "Now he can't get a decent night's rest."

"Neither can I," said Breslin. "I go home at the end of these shifts and try to get some shut-eye but I can't help wondering what's going through his mind when he screams and judders. Keeps me up."

Janikowski imagined Josh's night terrors were directly related to his fall, probably a byproduct of PTSD. Breslin thought that was for soldiers. "It can happen to anyone who's undergone a trauma. Going out a window and breaking one's back definitely qualifies."

Breslin wondered how that compared to committing three murders, but thought better of wondering it out loud. Instead he grinned and lifted his coffee cup. "Then I'll be getting them the rest of my life, thanks to this swill."

Janikowski was about to return the flirt when a spurt of high-pitched beeps clamored from a room around the corner. An alarm sounded over the ICU loudspeaker: Code Blue in room 1009. "Oh no, Mrs. Osborn!" Janikoswki rushed off to join a flurry of nurses and doctors headed for the code.

Breslin had never seen Janikowski in action, and didn't want to miss his chance. He took a last glance at Truffle, sleeping soundly, and loped after her. The ruckus went on, demanding the attention of all hands on deck.

No one saw the stranger enter Josh's room.

No one saw the stranger close the door and shut the blinds, as Cole had, too.

No one saw the stranger disconnect Josh's heart monitor. And because the ICU's medical staff was performing heroic measures to save Mrs. Osborn's life, no one was at the monitoring station to notice.

The stranger took out a small white packet of ammonia inhalant. "Time to rise and shine, Josh. I went to a lot of trouble to see you, even gave that old lady down the hall the wrong medication to make sure we wouldn't be disturbed." The stranger raised the packet to Josh's nostrils and broke it open. "Don't let her die in vain." The smelling salts' effect was almost instantaneous. Josh came to, his still-swollen eyes opened to slits.

"Was I having one of those fits?" he asked groggily. The stranger had moved opposite the bed to the television and inserted a DVD. It began to play.

"Nope. But this might do the trick."

"What is it?" Josh asked, woozy. "I can't see."

"I can help with that." The stranger produced two eye clamps, lifted from a storeroom, attached the first to the lids of

Josh's left eye, and spread, exposing Josh's crimson eye and holding it open. Josh screamed.

"It hurts!"

"That's the night terrors talking," soothed the stranger, who took hold of Josh's morphine drip and undammed it slightly. The drugs blanketed Josh as the stranger arranged the second eye clamp. "I thought you might appreciate a little clip show as I send you to your death. I think you'll really enjoy this one. It's your greatest hits. I pulled them right off Facebook."

Josh had nowhere to turn, nowhere to look, but the TV screen. On it, he saw himself. The stranger narrated. "Here you are at your eighth birthday party. You sure did like cake. What a scamp you were." The stranger turned up the morphine a notch. Josh tried to focus his googly eyes. There was a piñata that year. He'd moped when Cole broke it open first. "And here you are at eleven, on a class field trip to the zoo." Josh had liked the lions best. He'd roared at them. "This is fourteen. Swimming at Ben Feldman's. See how you and Cole and Scott dunked each other and played Marco Polo? Such friends, you used to be. What happened there?"

The stranger sat in a corner with the remote control, face veiled in shadow. The voice was familiar, though. Josh knew the voice from somewhere. "Who are you?" he asked.

The stranger supplied Josh with another bump of morphine. A bigger bump. "I feel like I'm floating away," he murmured.

"I bet you do," said the stranger. "Right down through the bowels of the earth. But stick with me. This is the best part. Here you are just a few months ago. At your favorite place in the whole wide world. The soccer field."

It was the first game of the season. Josh scored three goals without assistance. He dominated the defense. The visiting players hung their heads when it was over, while Josh's teammates lifted him into the air and carried him around, kinging him. It was the best feeling in the world, and he knew then it would go on forever.

"Now watch this," said the stranger. The team lowered Josh to the ground, where a nymph waited.

"That's Winnie," said Josh. She put her arms around him in the video and kissed him. In the bed, Josh opened his mouth to smile, forgetting that he'd pulverized most of his teeth in the fall, leaving only a few lonely white Chicklets. But the morphine made it okay. The morphine made everything okay. Even the fact that he couldn't close his eyes.

"I wanted you to see these things, Josh," said the stranger. "I wanted you to have one last look at the things you'd never again do or have or be. I wanted you to die knowing it was all stolen from you."

"Thank you," Josh whispered. "That's very kind. May I please . . ."

"May you please what?" asked the stranger.

"May I please have some more morphine?"

The stranger tittered. "You're a greedy one, aren't you?"

"Sorry."

"Don't be sorry," said the stranger. "You can have all the morphine you want." The stranger pushed Josh's morphine as far as it would go.

Josh watched the screen as a euphoric blessing threaded through him. Then his eyes rolled up into his head and his tired heart surrendered. A last breath hissed out, and with it, Winnie's name on his lips. The phantom stranger departed unseen, moments before the code team called an end to their efforts to save Mrs. Osborn's life.

When Breslin returned, the movie was paused on the soccer-field kiss Josh and Winnie shared. Caught in the background of the shot, to the other side and behind Winnie was one other person, staring out at the happy couple. He was out of focus and nearly unrecognizable to the uninitiated, but Josh knew him, and died looking at him.

Cole.

Josh Truffle

From *Wikipedia*, the free encyclopedia

Josh Truffle was an **American** high school student and aspiring soccer star. His dreams of World Cup tournaments, a personal line of sneaks, and shin-guard glory were dashed when his lifelong pattern of thievery was exposed. He stole girlfriends, grades, and prestige, and it was never enough. But it was all stolen away from him in the end.

He died never satisfied, always wanting more.

CHAPTER 29

It had grown late by the time Cole finished in the kitchen. He'd misjudged the time it would take to prepare his new variation on an old delight, but he was pleased with the results and knew the party would rage until whichever force arrived to break it up first, the crack of dawn or the police.

Cole stowed his treats in a bag, left a couple on a plate in the kitchen for his parents, and got to the business of escaping.

From his bedroom window Cole could see the police car squatting at the end of the street, dug in for the night. Cole picked up his phone and dialed 9-1-1.

"9-1-1, what is your emergency?" came the voice on the other end of the line.

"Hello, someone is sneaking through my backyard right now and it doesn't feel right." Cole gave an address several blocks away, in the direction opposite his route. "I'm not certain but I think it's a neighbor boy I've seen prowling around. Colton? Cole, maybe?" A moment later the call was relayed to the police car. It's lights and engine came to life. The driver pulled a one-eighty and took off. Cole knew the police would come to the house as soon as they couldn't track him down. His parents would insist he was asleep, but the police would insist on making sure. They'd find his bed empty and spread the word that a potential murder suspect was out and unaccounted for. It wouldn't take long for them to come looking at the party.

He had to book it.

Cole climbed out his window, adrenaline overpowering a queasy sensation that via window was not his body's preferred means of exit. He scaled the trellis, alit on the ground with nothing more than a thump, and took off through the night, submerged in a deepening freeze and swirling winds.

He heard the party coming long before he saw it. Muscular bass notes rocked the ground, sending vibrations up his legs as he emerged from the woods down the hill from Benito's and the vacant restaurant. The party was just gathering steam when Cole ran up, sweating icicles. Benito's had closed hours ago and the next-nearest structure was the empty high school, giving the revelry free reign for noise and devilry. Cars were parked up and down the road on either side, and more arrived by the minute, unpacking load after load of SHS students ready to channel the misery of the last few months into dance and drama.

Cole scouted the perimeter of the restaurant, and felt eyes on him in return. The spectacle with Winnie and Josh had endowed him with an edge that drew sometimes jealous, sometimes horny stares. But there was another kind of watchfulness in the crowd. Somewhere in the cliques, ebbing and flowing into the restaurant and out of it, a person monitored with sinister intent. The hair on the back of his neck stood on end and he simmered goose bumps. Cole's body knew how this hidden stare looked at him without his head even having to think it.

He was quarry.

His observer melted into the crowds, unrevealed. The feeling passed, but Cole knew it would be back again, and soon. He tried to swallow his fear but found he had no saliva. He'd had nerves before. This was different. This was knowing a target was painted on his back, and soon a knife might be sunk into it, too.

It would help if he didn't feel so alone among the sea of faces. Gavin was nowhere in sight. Maybe he was inside already, busting out his best head bop. Cole readied himself and headed for the entrance.

Someone touched his shoulder.

Lila.

"Finally," he breathed. "I was looking all over."

"I've been here," she said. "Waiting for you."

Cole apologized. "No car." Tonight Lila wore red coveralls under a plaid peacoat and train conductor's cap. The clash was disorienting. "At least I won't mistake someone else for you."

"Are you going to tell me what we're doing here?" She shivered as the wind pushed through her coat. "Besides freezing our *Arsches* off?"

Cole kept his voice down and his eyes up, on the lookout, as he spilled his guts.

Lila stared at him, slack-jawed. "Do you actually believe this?"

Cole nodded solemnly.

Lila computed. "It would make for a banging story. If it's true."

"It's a pretty good story if it isn't true, too. 'Valedictorian Descends into Madness and Paranoia,' or whatever. Either way, the exclusive is yours. But I need help. I need backup." He could do better than that. "I need you."

"I'll say." She added, "Among other things."

This was banter. This was promising. "So? What do you think?"

"I think you're crazy not to call the police," she said slowly. "But I understand why you haven't. And I do believe I'm honored you called an intrepid reporter instead."

Cole took this for agreement. "Did you bring the recorder?"

Lila removed her hand from her jacket. "I brought two. One for you and one for me."

"Perfect. Turn yours on, put it in your pocket, and forget it's there." Cole did the same with his, then held out his hand.

"What's that for?" Lila asked.

"I owe you a date, remember?"

"I don't hold hands with killers. Much less date them." But she hadn't moved.

"Then you're safe with me," said Cole.

"Actually, I think I'd be a lot safer at home right now." She held his look for a moment, then took his hand. He wrapped his fingers around hers. *Check that out,* came an unexpected thought, *they fit.* He shivered against the wind. "You ready?"

Lila shrugged. "Not really. Does it matter?"

It didn't. There could be no more delay.

He grasped her hand tighter, led her to the party, and plunged in.

CHAPTER 30

The light and heat slapped them both at once.

A rainbow of laser lights zigzagged across the dance floor, intermittently bathing the dancing zombie teenagers in blues, greens, and reds. The only other light came from a powerful, unyielding strobe that transformed the party into a bad stop-motion animation film.

And the heat.

It shouldn't have been so hot inside.

The restaurant had been empty for years since Cole shut it down, the gas and electricity shut off after disuse. Not even the steam heat of the hundreds of gyrating dancers layered front to back and back to front on the dance floor could have insulated the building against the fast-dropping temperature outside the makeshift dance floor. Lila felt it, too, and pointed at something running along the baseboard.

Space heaters, hooked up to a portable generator. Cole was amazed not one of them had been knocked over and caught fire.

"This place is a death trap," Lila yelled.

"What?" Cole screamed back. He couldn't understand her over the din of the speakers and the clatter of the generator. The music was so loud, the beat so potent, that he felt as if it was spreading out from inside him.

"I said this place is a death trap!"

Cole shook his head. "I can't understand you!" Somehow,

that didn't stop him from attempting to communicate by yelling over the noise.

Lila did her best to mime. *Just be careful.*

Cole thought he understood. *Keep away from the space heaters.*

"Hang on tight," he said. "Let's hit the dance floor." Lila was mystified. Cole did his best "Single Ladies" impression. Lila went white and backed off. Cole pulled her into the writhing horde anyway, feeling a familiar tightness across his face, a sensation he'd almost forgotten.

A smile.

Cole pushed through the scrum, getting up close and personal with a lot of guys and girls who minded, and a lot who didn't. He pulled Lila along behind him like a wagon, but the deeper they ventured, the thicker, less clothed, and slicker the crowd became, and that much harder to navigate. Cole slid between bodies, redoubling his grip on her slippery fingers. His eyes were peeled for Gavin, and his instincts extended like antennae, sensing for signs of his would-be killer.

But the restaurant was too dark to see more than one dancer deep. And it was ripe with too much sound and odor and skin to tell where one body ended and the next began.

Cole began to reconsider the merits of his plan. There were too many people. Too many variables. Too much could go wrong.

There was a shout from behind him and above.

Lila dug her fingernails into his wrist and he whirled.

A football player, a six-feet-tall-and-two-hundred-pound slab of shirtless, hairy offensive line had climbed on top of the restaurant's bar. Arms of countless dancers below him rose up and stretched out. The one-man demolition derby bent at the knees.

Oh no, thought Cole.

The lumpy lineman sprung into the air with impressive grace and gave himself to the mercy of the crowd.

They had none to give.

His girth brushed aside the arms that would have held him up as if they were bendy straws. He landed across Cole and Lila's fingerlock, violently breaking them apart as he pancaked the people between them. Nature abhors a vacuum and so do dancers; immediately more bodies rushed to claim the places of those who were still struggling to get to their feet. Lila was engulfed in the thicket. He lost sight of her.

Cole tried to head in her direction but met with a wall of bodies. He spun from one direction to the next, heart pounding and sweat pooling, the strobe cutting in and out, throwing him off course.

He couldn't see her. But he had to find her. He couldn't leave her on her own, wrapped up in a mess of his own making, just like he'd done to Winnie. He couldn't let history repeat itself.

He wouldn't.

Cole pointed himself back in the direction from which he thought he'd come and hurled himself at the first group of dancers standing in his way. They pitched backward. He'd made a hole.

He revved up to do it again, but froze.

On the other side of the space he'd created was Gavin, kissing a girl, her back turned to Cole. Cole couldn't see her face, but he knew who she was.

Gavin broke from her kiss and leaned down to whisper something in her ear but stopped when he saw Cole staring back.

The look in Gavin's eye seemed friendly and welcoming.

But Cole knew he was as welcome as a fly in a spiderweb.

CHAPTER 31

Cole's stomach warped.

His best friend since T-ball and graham crackers stood just a few feet away. But Cole had never felt so far apart from him. Gavin said something to the girl clinging to his shirt just as another surge of partiers rushed into the space between them, masking Cole's view. He squished through, popping out onto the other side. Gavin stood there waiting and nodding to the music. The girl was gone.

"You're still alive, I see," Gavin yelled in Cole's ear. His grin gleamed. "It's getting close to midnight, too. I think it's safe to say you've survived your Wikipedia entry."

There's still time, Cole thought. "What happened to your friend?"

"What friend?" asked Gavin.

"The one you were kissing just now."

Gavin pursed his lips and shrugged dispassionately, like a player. "She's not a friend. What's in the bag?"

Cole almost forgot he had it. "I made Rice Krispies Treats. But I don't think anyone's hungry."

Gavin crossed his eyes in mock offense. "Don't you know me at all?" asked Gavin. *It would seem not. Is Gavin really even your name?* Cole thought. "I can always eat. Come on, I know a quieter spot."

Cole trailed Gavin through the party, ramming dancers out

of the way when he had to. He craned his head around and around, skimming the restaurant for a trace of Lila. There was no sign of her. Maybe she'd gone outside for a breather. Maybe.

He caught up to Gavin behind the bar. More crowd surfers had climbed on top and were launching themselves. "Where are we going?"

"Through here," Gavin said, dipping down and disappearing. The outline of a hatch in the floor flickered in the strobe light. Cole hesitated.

If he went into that hole and things went bad, he might never come back out.

Winnie was dead. Scott was dead. Drick was dead. Cole owed it to them to keep going. He looked one last time for Lila but she failed to appear. He would just have to live and find her later.

He stooped, opened the door, and began to carefully climb down a flight of stairs in pitch black.

"Gavin? Where'd you go?"

Cole put his hands out and felt the walls of the stairwell on either side. He took a trembling step down. And then another. The noise of the party muffled above him with each step forward, and other sounds came into focus. The stairs creaking beneath him. The rough scratch of sawdust sliding against the soles of his shoes. What he hoped very much were not the bones of small dead rodents.

"Gavin, come on already —"

"BOO!" A bright light shot out of the dark, one step below Cole. His feet fell out from under him and he fell backward, sitting back on the stairs. Gavin's flashlight app was aimed upward at his face from beneath his chin. He laughed like a cartoon Dracula. "Scare ya?"

Down to his molecules. "Where are we going?"

Gavin waved. "We're here."

A few more steps and they materialized in a large open basement. Gavin's phone light threw off enough glow that Cole could identify a dusty walk-in freezer, empty cobwebbed kegs, and high, bare shelves. Stationed around the space were a few worktables equipped with basic tools. A hammer here, a vise there.

"Better, huh?" Gavin asked.

"Lots," said Cole, his eyes adjusting to the murk. "Couldn't hear myself think up there."

"That's the whole point of a party like this. Give everyone an excuse to stop thinking and shut off our brains for a while," Gavin said.

"I wish I could shut mine off," Cole mused. "It just keeps going. It just keeps asking questions."

Gavin snorted. "Better be careful," he warned in singsong. "That could get you in trouble." But Cole knew he was already well beyond that point. "So let's see what you've got in there," Gavin said, gesturing at Cole's bag. "Papa's famished."

So was Cole. He was hungry for answers and had waited, been lied to and toyed with long enough. "When were you going to tell me, Gavin?"

Gavin hopped up on a table and swung his feet. Left, right. Left, right. The light from his phone cast misshapen, grotesque shadows all over the room. "Still with the questions? Fine. If that's the way you want it." He tsked. His voice was soft and laced with menace. "But you'll have to be more specific than that. There are so many things to choose from. When was I going to tell you what?"

Cole had come this far. He would see it through.

"That you killed Scott. And Drick." He took another breath. "And Winnie."

Gavin stopped swinging his feet. Cole couldn't see his eyes, hooded in shadow, but his half-moon grin was clear. "Honestly? I was hoping I wouldn't have to. I wasn't sure I could. I've found that ending a life is surprisingly easy. Once you get the hang of it, at least." He plucked a piece of lint from his sleeve and flicked it. "But disappointing someone you care about? Someone whose opinion matters to you? That's hard. I guess I'm a coward that way. But now that it's happening, I'm glad. This is better."

"Better, why?"

"Because you're my best friend," Gavin pledged. It was the ugliest thing he'd ever said to Cole. Then he managed to top himself. He reached inside his jacket. When he removed his hand, he was holding a nasty-looking knife. "And as my best friend, you have the right to know everything. I owe you the truth before I kill you."

CHAPTER 32

When did you start to figure it out?" asked Gavin, back to swinging his legs like a hyperactive, homicidal five-year-old.

Cole was still stuck back on the part about Gavin killing him, and the blade he wielded, glinting in the light of his phone. Cole felt the recorder in his pocket, silently soaking up their conversation. He could take off right now, grab Lila, go to the cops, and play them what Gavin had just said. But would that be enough? Gavin could claim it was all a joke. Cole needed to extract the full story or this would be for nothing.

"Come on, humor me," Gavin prodded.

"Humor you?" Cole sputtered. "You said you're going to kill me."

Gavin cocked his head tenderly. "Are you worried it'll hurt? I promise to be gentle for my best friend."

"Stop saying that," Cole spat. "You are not my best friend. I don't know what you are."

"A guy who likes to learn from his mistakes, among other things. Are you going to tell me what gave me away? Or should we skip the truth-telling bit and go straight to the good-byes?"

"Harry Styles. Happy?"

Gavin raised an eyebrow. "Come again?"

"Your One Direction love match. You told me so yourself. You took the quiz in the Taylor Swift issue of *Teen Vogue*.

I found a copy of the magazine with your answers circled in Josh's hospital room. It had a mailing label addressed to Andrea on it."

Cole could see Gavin's tongue swirl around beneath his cheek as he worked it out. "If you don't mind my saying, that's pretty thin," said Gavin, dubious. "What could you have even gotten from that? That Andrea and I were secretly seeing each other? So what?"

"You were the last piece of the puzzle. Andrea was the first."

"Girls," Gavin clucked. "I'm discovering they're more trouble than they're worth."

"Well your taste could use some refining."

Gavin deflated. "Watch it. If you aren't nice, I won't be nice. The same way we weren't nice to her father."

"You killed Mr. Henderson, too?"

"He never took a shine to me. Can you believe it? Apparently he has something against wit and devilish good looks."

"Or maybe he has something against murder," Cole guessed.

"He was threatening to send Andrea away to boarding school if she didn't dump me," Gavin said. "What were we supposed to do, off ourselves like some modern basic cable adaptation of *Romeo and Juliet*? Better to kill him than kill ourselves. He had to go around in secret while we came up with the plan to make him our test subject."

"That must have been a giant sacrifice," Cole said.

"Enough with the comedy. Tell me when you picked up Andrea's trail?"

"It was when I saw Josh in the hospital. He let on that she'd been in touch with him while he was hiding from the cops. She made him think he still had a chance with Winnie even though she was already trying to get back together with me. Andrea steered him to Winnie's house at the exact moment I was there finding her body."

"The timing was too coincidental for you?" Gavin gave him a smug look.

"She gave herself away. I knew she was involved somehow, but I didn't know how deep it got. I didn't even know if she'd killed Winnie because I was positive she wasn't acting alone. She'd been in the hospital when Drick was killed. Recovering from a near-fatal experience with contaminated eyedrops. Just like her Wikipedia entry."

"That must've been confusing."

"That was no bad batch of chronic dry eye medication. And she didn't do it to herself on purpose. You spiked it, didn't you?"

Gavin held a finger to his lips. "She doesn't need to know that."

"How could you blind your own girlfriend?"

"Let's be clear. She can still see out of one eye, and she's not technically blind in the other eye because she doesn't even have that eye anymore. The acid melted it clean away. Nothing but socket left there. So we're not even approaching a Helen Keller situation. And I didn't mean for her to lose her whole eye. I swiped the wrong kind of acid from chemistry. It was Diet-Coke-and-Mentos Day in class and I got a little distracted. Sue me."

"But why risk it at all?"

"Because of how much I respect your deductive capabilities," Gavin said, ever patient. "You might have found it curious if terrible things happened to all your Wikipedia targets except her. And I couldn't chance you connecting us."

"So you killed Drick yourself."

"Had to," said Gavin. "You were on your way to see him and spill your guts. I knew as soon as you told him what you'd been up to he'd go straight to the cops, like any sensible person would. They'd take one look at the pages and come knocking on your door."

"So? All the pages were made on my computer. You had plausible deniability. Even after I'd deleted the entries, they'd been restored using my log-in and password."

"You can thank Chetley for that one. He taught me the finer points of hacking in the early days of Protest Club, when we thought we were anarchists. We brainstormed breaking into the school's grading files and giving everyone straight As," said Gavin.

"But you could've sent me up the river right then," Cole persisted. "Why did you have to kill Winnie?"

"Because it made for a better story."

Cole didn't understand.

Gavin sighed. "Allow me to explain. What's your GPA?"

Cole wrinkled his brow. "What does that have to do with anything?"

"Just answer the question."

"I don't know what it is," he said honestly. "High. High enough to be valedictorian."

"So high that you don't even pay attention," said Gavin, shaking his head. "That's luxury. Plus you've got all kinds of honors and awards and extracurriculars up the yin-yang. You've got it made. You'll go to any school you want and have a really extraordinary life. While I sit around Springfield flipping burgers.

"I know, I know," Gavin admitted. "You don't have to say it. I screwed up. It's my own fault. I'd be in an okay position now if I'd applied myself like you did. But I didn't. I slacked off and mouthed off and didn't pay attention to what my life would turn out to be like after graduation until senior year arrived and I found out it was too late to get what you're going to have.

"At least not by conventional means."

"What are you getting at?" asked Cole.

"I lost my chance to fatten up my transcript with grades and distinctions. But I can write a mean essay. Just think of all the schools that'll beat down my door when I write the story of how I brought to justice my best friend, mass murderer Cole Redeker."

Cole felt his ribs buckle.

"I have a first draft at home," said Gavin, swelling with pride. "I'm sorry I don't have a copy with me to read to you, but I'll boil it down. The second option on the common application prompt goes like this: 'Recount an incident or time when you experienced failure. How did it affect you, and what lessons did you learn?'

"Well my failure would be in letting my deep and abiding love for my best friend blind me from seeing that he'd gone on a killing spree. I tell the story of how I became increasingly concerned about your mental well-being after Winnie dumped you for Josh. I describe your behavior becoming more and more erratic, but that I chalk it up to stress over grades and applying to college. I mention stumbling onto a strange Wikipedia page on your computer one day. It was an entry for a classmate of ours, Scott Dare, and it recounted his gruesome death — only he wasn't dead . . . yet. That would soon change. I delve into my investigation, tracking down other Wikipedia pages, matching them to still more suspicious deaths, and realizing all the pages were written before the deaths even occurred, and all of them written by the same person — my best friend, Cole Redeker! I recount the pain and horror of making this discovery, the tears I shed trying to get him to turn himself in . . . and the awful day when he turned on me."

Gavin held the knife up.

"I describe in painstaking detail fighting desperately for my life against a guy who killed a classmate, a teacher, his own girlfriend, her new boyfriend — oh, did I forget to mention I put Josh out of his misery before the party? I put Josh out of his misery before the party. Plus one other . . . the fetching student reporter who had begun her own independent investigation of the run of blood."

"If you touch Lila, I swear to God, I'll kill you," Cole promised.

"How very chilling, Cole. But I'm the one with the knife."

Cole pulled out the recorder. "True. But I'm the one with the confession."

CHAPTER 33

Cole played back the last few moments of Gavin's monologue and silently prayed to God for salvation — yes, he believed in God now and would continue to do so if only he got out of this alive, amen. Even in the limited light, Cole could see the color drain from Gavin's face as his digitized voice came to a halt. "Wow."

"Yeah," said Cole, edging backward toward the stairs, "wow. Pretty damning, don't you think?"

Gavin suddenly seemed unfazed. "No, I meant, 'Wow, is that what I really sound like?' I thought I had a deeper voice."

"I think you have other things to worry about rather than which part you'll play in the prison choir." Cole wasn't going to let Gavin have all the good lines.

"I'm not going to prison," Gavin insisted, entertained by Cole's silly certainty. "I'm going to college. A good college. Someplace where they reward independence and freewheelers! Oberlin, or Bard, or Sarah Lawrence! You, on the other hand, are going to die."

Gavin turned off his cell phone flashlight.

The basement was swamped in black. Cole instinctively dropped to a crouch and balled himself tight, just as Gavin's shins slammed into him. Cole felt Gavin somersault over and hit the concrete floor with a *thwack*. A skidding, clattering sound announced that the knife was up for grabs somewhere, but Cole opted not to linger and grope for it. Gavin was groaning very close by, and might regroup soon.

Cole scrabbled backward until he bumped into the staircase, turned, and took the stairs on his stomach, crabbing up to the top.

Below, Gavin chimed, "Wait! I didn't get my Rice Krispies Treat!"

Cole could not fathom why Gavin sounded so unconcerned about the prospect of imminent arrest, but he could not bring himself to care. He sprang out of the basement and into the party, which had only grown louder and more crowded in his absence. He turned around and threw the hatch back down, looking for a lock or a chair or a box, anything he could use to secure Gavin inside, but there were only dancers. Suddenly the hatch pressed up from within and Cole saw Gavin's head begin to emerge. Holding the knife, he reached his hand out through the crack and stabbed at Cole's foot. But Cole was faster.

He raised his leg and stamped his foot down, flattening the hatch against the floor. Gavin's arm was momentarily crushed between the hatch and the floor, and he pulled it back inside. Cole grabbed the nearest pair of students, yanked them over and stood them on the hatch, then jumped on top of the bar.

The revelers nearest to him on the dance floor lifted their arms up and beckoned and bopped.

Behind him, the dancers pitched as Gavin pushed on the hatch with all his might. Cole looked out onto the dance floor.

There, in the center of the room, amidst the breeding ball of dancers and uplifted arms, was a girl in a plaid peacoat and train conductor's cap. She was headed away from him in the direction of the exit. Cole cupped his mouth and screamed.

"LILA!"

She kept going, unable to hear him over the din.

He risked a glance behind him. The hatch dancers were on

their butts, knocked over. Gavin rose from the depths, knife at the ready.

Cole chucked himself off the bar and sailed.

And landed in a net of palms.

The dancers cheered and conducted him away from the center of the room.

Cole turned his head as he was wormed away and spied Gavin scaling the bar.

As soon as Cole was within scrambling range of the door, he swept his legs out from behind him, kicking faces as he went.

"Sorry!" he called back as he got his feet under him and bounced for the door.

Outside, the early winter wind lashed at Cole's face as he swept his eyes across the property. He caught a glimpse of the conductor's cap as Lila rounded a corner, disappearing behind Benito's.

"Lila, wait!"

Cole streaked through the clusters of students and swung around behind Benito's, catching up to Lila just as she put her hand on the back door's knob. Out of the corner of his eye Cole noticed that one of the glass windowpanes on the top half of the door was broken. *Benito's going to have a fit about that,* he thought.

Cole took Lila by the shoulder and turned her around.

"Lila, we have to get out of —"

The girl before him was dressed in Lila's coat and cap, but she was not wearing Lila's red coveralls. She did, however, wear a black eye patch over one eye.

"My name isn't Lila, Cole," purred Andrea.

A sharp pain glanced across the back of Cole's head.

Not again was his last thought before the nothingness took him.

CHAPTER 34

Cole came to amidst a screaming match.

Whatever knocked him out this time could not have been as strong as either of the first two blows that concussed him. His bell still rung, but this time he had no trouble identifying the voices of those speaking.

"I still don't understand why you brought her here!" yelled Gavin.

"What was I supposed to do with her?" Andrea shrieked. "Drag her unconscious through the party to your little lair in the basement? Don't you think that might have been a little conspicuous?"

A third voice made itself known in the form of a hitched sob.

"Please let me go. Please."

Lila.

Cole opened his eyes. His gaze landed first on a white piece of paper on a wall. Written on it in black marker were the words *IF YOUR NAME ISN'T COLE YOU DON'T SIT HERE.*

Benito's.

"Could you not have put her in the trunk of your car? We have now officially broken into and entered Benito's. Our fingerprints are everywhere. How are we going to explain this?"

Something was very, very wrong with Cole.

"I'm sure you'll think of something," prickled Andrea. "After all, you are the mad genius."

He was on his knees at the end of his booth, facing the table. His mouth was open and his chin jammed against the table's lip. He could not move his head and his mind required one moment of clear thought to process why.

"Now can we please get this over with?" harped Andrea. "Before someone catches on?"

Cole's tongue had been stretched from his mouth and laid flat on the table. A metal vise clamped down on the tip, immobilizing it against the table.

Cole tried to scream. The sound was garbled and choked.

"Look who's decided to join us," said Gavin.

Lila cried out from the counter. "Cole, he has a knife!"

Cole could just barely grab a glimpse of Lila in his peripheral vision. She was up on the counter, flat on her back, her hair fed into the gears of Benito's manual pasta roller. It was bolted to the table. She clawed at her hair and tugged, trying to free herself.

She was going nowhere, and neither was he.

Gavin sidled up to Cole. "You know what my first order of business is going to be when you are dead and buried? I'm going to rip down that sign that I am forced to look at every time I sit down here. And a new sign is going up. *IF YOUR NAME ISN'T GAVIN YOU DON'T SIT HERE.*"

"Any day now," badgered Andrea. "I really want to go home and wash my hair and clean out my socket. My glass eye is coming tomorrow and I want to look good."

"We'll be done in two shakes of a lamb's tail," said Gavin, turning to Cole. "Isn't she great?" He rested the knife at Cole's throat. "Now I know I said this wasn't going to hurt. . . ."

Cole had two seconds to save his life, and two weapons at his disposal. Next to him, on the booth seat, was his bag of Rice Krispies Treats. He grabbed them and held them up to Gavin.

"What's this, dude?" asked Gavin. "A peace offering?"

Cole found that he could manage some vowels without the use of his tongue. "Uh-huh."

Gavin twinkled. "Don't mind if I do." He reached in and pulled out a big, honking treat. "But I still gotta kill ya."

He opened his mouth and took a big bite.

Cole reached into his pocket and slipped out the recorder, dialed it back a few minutes.

"Man, this is delicious," raved Gavin. "What is the world going to do without your stove-top sorcery?" He swallowed and took another bite as Cole hit PLAY.

Cole's voice drifted out of the recorder, and then Gavin's. Andrea perked up.

Cole: That was no bad batch of chronic dry eye medication. And she didn't do it to herself on purpose. You spiked it, didn't you?

"What is that?" Andrea asked. Gavin froze.

Gavin: She doesn't need to know that.

Gavin coughed as he reached for the recorder. Cole tossed it deeper into the booth.

"Did YOU say that?" Andrea demanded.

Cole: How could you blind your own girlfriend?

Gavin crawled into the booth but Andrea leapt on top of him, beating his back.

"I WANT TO HEAR IT! I WANT TO HEAR WHAT YOU DID TO ME!"

"Fine," Gavin wheezed, relinquishing the recorder. "Listen to all you want."

Andrea prized the recorder as Gavin's confession unrolled.

Gavin: Let's be clear. She can still see out of one eye, and she's not technically blind in the other eye because she doesn't even have that eye anymore. The acid melted it clean away. Nothing but socket left there. So we're not even approaching a Helen Keller situation. And I didn't mean for her to lose her whole eye. I swiped the wrong kind of acid from chemistry. It was Diet-Coke-and-Mentos Day in class and I got a little distracted. Sue me.

Andrea faced Gavin, crying from her one eye.

"How could you?"

"Easily," Gavin cackled. "Just like this." In one simple, casual gesture, he flicked his knife into her belly and drew it up to her sternum. Lila screamed and Andrea gurgled, toppling over. Organs flopped out from the wound, red-brown and steamy as she splatted on the floor. Her knife fell from her grasp and spun within Cole's reach. Gavin coughed harder.

"Cole, is this a new recipe?"

"Uh-huh," came Cole's distorted response as he retrieved Andrea's knife. "Kee hireen ith heeutt uhuh."

Gavin played the translation in his head, then squealed. "Peanut butter?"

Cole lifted the knife to his tongue and cleared his mind's eye, focusing on the technique he'd learned at a summer intensive cooking course. With one firm flick, he sliced the blade across the end of his tongue, severing just the very tip.

Lila was struck silent as Cole rose to his feet as if on choppy seas. Blood cascaded down his chin as he pocketed his tongue and moved to cut Lila free of her tangled hair.

Gavin blubbered on the floor. Peanut allergens paraded through his body, laying waste. One swollen hand scraped at his inflated throat, as if to tear a new airway. The other hand dug at his pocket, where Cole knew he kept an EpiPen. But his hand had become the size and shape of a foot. It would not fit.

Cole freed Lila. "Your mouth," she said. "Hospital? Hospital." They turned to face Gavin. A whistle escaped his lips. Cole walked over and shoved his hand in Gavin's pocket and held up the EpiPen. Gavin looked up at him, suffocated by his own throat. Cole broke the pen in half and dropped it on Gavin, then walked out with Lila, into the night.

Cole Redeker

From *Wikipedia*, the free encyclopedia

Cole Redeker is an **American** college student whose attempt to get even with a high school rival set off a chain reaction that resulted in a murder spree dubbed "The Wickedpedia Killings."[1] Redeker uncovered the identity of the Wickedpedia killer but nearly died, losing the tip of his tongue in the process. He declined acceptance to Harvard and Yale to purse a degree from the Culinary Institute of America, where he is thought to be the first prospective graduate to lack the ability to taste sweetness.

In his spare time, Redeker studies the German language.

He drives a Kia.

[1] See article on **Gavin Peters**.

READY FOR MORE SCARES?

WE DARE YOU TO CHECK OUT THESE OTHER CHILLING TALES!

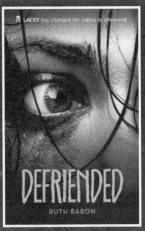

Defriended
by Ruth Baron

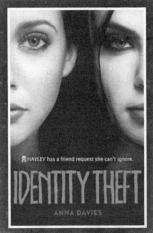

Identity Theft
by Anna Davies

Followers
by Anna Davies

Wickedpedia
by Chris Van Etten

POINT HORROR